ARTHUR J. BECKHARD is the author of several biographies of famous world figures. He attended The Ethical Culture School, Amherst College, and the Columbia School of Journalism. Beckhard has worked as a free-lance feature writer, crime reporter, music and drama critic, and editorial writer. He has also worked as a concert manager and a Broadway producer-director. His first book was THE STORY OF DWIGHT D. EISENHOWER. Since then he has written other biographies, including BLACK HAWK; ELECTRICAL GENIUS: NIKOLA TESLA; CANCER, COCAINE AND COURAGE: THE STORY OF DR. WILLIAM HALSTED. The cover photograph on this edition is by Philippe Halsman.

ALBERT EINSTEIN

ARTHUR BECKHARD

CAMELOT

AN AVON CAMELOT book

AVON BOOKS
A division of
The Hearst Corporation
959 Eighth Avenue
New York, New York 10019

Published by arrangement with G. P. Putnam's Sons.

First Avon Printing, August, 1960
Fourth Avon Printing, September, 1963
First Avon Camelot Printing (Fifth Printing), September, 1966

Printed in the U.S.A.

CONTENTS

ALBERT EINSTEIN

Chapter 1

CHASING THE "X"

"WHY DO I have to go to school, Papa?"

Hermann Einstein, tall and severe-looking, looked down at his ten-year-old son. "Do you want to grow up to be an ignoramus, Albert?"

"What's an ignoramus?"

A burst of laughter came from a corner of the large, comfortably furnished living room. Father and son turned quickly toward Mrs. Einstein, who was seated at the large black piano.

"Oh Hermann," Mrs. Einstein exclaimed, her voice still bubbling with laughter, "you'll never beat Albert at that game!"

"I'm sure I don't know what you mean," her husband sputtered.

"There's no use in pretending," Mrs. Einstein replied, as she went on playing an old Hungarian folk song. "I heard you and your brother deciding that the only way to keep Albert from asking so many questions was to answer him by asking *him* a question. But you see—it didn't work. He can always outlast you!"

Albert crossed the room and stood beside his mother, for a moment forgetting what he had asked. Her fingers fascinated him. They were such stubby, soft little fingers, and yet they danced and fluttered across the keys with the speed of a robin running across the lawn. They hit the keys so firmly, without fumbling or hesitation, that they made the piano fairly sing. They leaped and pounced upon two final crashing chords. Mrs. Einstein swung herself around on the piano bench and took Albert into her arms.

She looked over the top of his dark, curly head and smiled up at her husband. "You see, there *is* a way to make Albert stop asking questions. My music will do it."

Mr. Einstein nodded, smiling. Before he had a chance to answer, Albert wriggled around in his mother's arms so that he could turn and face her.

"Is it wrong to ask questions?" he asked.

Now it was Mr. Einstein's turn to laugh.

"There he goes again!" He chuckled. "Even your music can't stop him for long."

Mrs. Einstein looked at her husband reprovingly, and she gave Albert a small hug.

"There's nothing wrong in asking questions, *Liebchen,*" she said fondly, "as long as you don't do it just to tease or embarrass people or to make them seem foolish."

"I don't do it like that," the boy protested. "I do it because there is so much I don't know—so much I want to know. I want to know all about everything—right away."

Albert's mother smiled proudly, but his father drew his heavy eyebrows together. He looked puzzled.

"If you really mean that, Albert, how is it that you could ask why you must go to school? School is the place where questions should be answered."

"But they're not!" Albert cried out. "They don't even let anybody ask questions, and they'd never think of answering them. I hate school. It's like being in prison. The teachers are like prison guards marching up and down between the rows of desks."

Mr. Einstein and his lovely wife exchanged a look that was full of meaning. What could they say in answer to their son's charges?

This was the year 1889 in Munich, Germany. Less than five years before, Bismarck, the great German militarist, had conquered all of Bavaria along with several other small countries that had always been free and independent, and formed them all into one country which he called Prussia. The Einsteins had moved from the little city of Ulm, in Bavaria, in 1880, a year after Albert was born. Mr. Einstein and his brother Jacob, who had foreseen what would happen to Bavaria, had packed up and brought the whole family to Munich. There the two brothers set up a small chemist's shop. They had been there only a year when Albert's little sister, Maja, was born, and the family moved into a large, comfortable house just outside the center of town.

It was not long before "the Einstein House," as people called it, became one of the most popular places in the whole city of Munich. Often when permanent residents had guests from out of town they took them to the Einstein House for an evening of conversation and music or poetry reading. These evenings were so much discussed that often visitors to Munich would, upon arrival, ask their hosts if they could possibly arrange for an invitation to the Einsteins'.

An invitation, however, was scarcely necessary. There was nothing formal about these affairs. Sometimes Mrs. Einstein would play Mozart or Brahms compositions. Sometimes she would sing the folk ballads of Germany and Austria. On some evenings, the guests all gathered around the piano and sang old songs they all knew. Both Mr. Einstein and his brother had deep pleasant voices and could lead their guests in these familiar melodies.

Many times neighbors and friends gathered just to talk in the warm, friendly living room with its deep maroon wallpaper lighted by the orange glow from the gaslight chandelier that hung from the white ceiling, and the evening sped by without allowing time for any music at all. Young Albert hated to go to bed on these occasions. He listened, wide-eyed, to the talk of new inventions like the electric light and the telephone. His father and Uncle Jacob were well posted on all the latest scientific developments, particularly those which might affect the sale of equipment and the electro-chemical apparatus. Their shop was far ahead of their competitors in all such matters.

There were times when Albert's father would decide to read aloud from the works of great German writers such as Goethe, Schiller and Heinrich Heine. Young Albert could never decide which kind of evening at home he liked best. Certainly there was a great contrast between learning in the friendly atmosphere of his own home and the austere school classrooms where the pupils were punished for failure but never given praise or encouragement for accomplishments.

Mr. and Mrs. Einstein spent a good deal of thought in the selection of a school for Albert. He had been backward as a small child, slow to learn to talk and read and very shy. They had selected a Catholic school considered the very best in Munich. They were dismayed when the government took over the operation of all the schools and began installing military rules and regulations.

"The true culture of Germany is being submerged by militarism," Mr. Einstein exclaimed sadly.

But neither of Albert's parents had realized the extent to which the Prussian army had taken over the public school system until Albert's very real unhappiness became apparent to them.

"They make us memorize the day's lesson," the boy told them. "They don't tell us what it says or what it means, but we must learn every single word. And I can't. Unless I know what a thing means I just can't remember it. And so they open the drawer and take out the ruler. . . ."

His mother hugged him and kissed the palm of his hand, still red from the strokes of the steel ruler. She looked up at her husband appealingly. Mr. Einstein shook his head.

"There's nothing we can do," he said. "They will question our loyalty if we complain to the principal." He sat down and beckoned Albert to come closer.

"Albert," he said, placing a friendly hand on his son's shoulder, "your mother and I don't like this any more than you do, but we must all face it. You are old enough now to understand what is going on in the world around you. The army is becoming more and more important in Germany and in Austria. It will not be long before the army rules the country. Even now, army officers are buying up big businesses. So far they have bought only the larger stores. But soon they will see that Mr. So-and-so has a nice little candy store on the corner. They will buy the store across the street. Then they will tell everyone that they must stop buying candy from Mr. So-and-so and must, instead, buy from the new store. That is the way it usually works out when the military becomes too important.

"The real reason why you must go to school is that there is a law in Germany that no one may get a job unless he has a diploma. You will have to finish six more years of primary school and high school before you can get one; and some day you may have to get a job and help me and Uncle Jacob support your mother and little Maja."

Albert looked into his father's face and saw that he was not fooling. The situation was serious.

"I won't complain any more, Father," he said. "I'll try my best to get along in school."

Then he turned and, with his head lowered, eyes staring at the flower pattern in the carpet, he started toward the door. In the doorway he turned.

"Perhaps I could earn money playing my violin," he said. "Then I wouldn't have to have a diploma."

"I'm afraid you would have to practice a long time to learn to play well enough to have people pay to hear you," his mother said, as if she were considering the possibility in all seriousness.

"I wouldn't mind practicing if I knew why," Albert explained. "And I don't mind it any more—"

"Albert," his father interrupted, "I don't think it would be a good idea. It's never a good idea to do something you love doing just for money. It always spoils it."

"What's that? What's that I hear?" a big voice shouted from the little foyer just outside the living room. It was Uncle Jacob.

"Hermann, did I hear you telling the boy that it was wrong to get money for doing a job you enjoy? That's poppycock and you know it!"

Uncle Jacob was a big man, much taller and heavier than Albert's father; his booming voice always seemed to carry a great deal of authority. Now he turned to Albert and addressed him with all the seriousness of a defense attorney pleading his client's case before a judge and jury.

"My boy, try to understand what I'm saying. You should always try to do work you love. And if you find yourself in a spot where you have to do work that you dislike, you must find a way of making yourself like it so that you can do it well."

Albert looked doubtful. He shook his head. "I hate school," he said stubbornly.

"Albert!" Mr. Einstein said severely. "I don't want you to use that word. There is enough hate in the world without hating such a thing as schoolwork."

He lapsed into silence as Mrs. Einstein put a quieting hand on his arm. Uncle Jacob crossed over to the fireplace and lifted his long porcelain-bowl pipe off the mantel.

"I think I can show you what I mean, boy," he said. "What subject do you 'hate' the most?"

Albert thought for a moment before answering.

"I can't decide between algebra and geometry. I hate—I mean I dislike them both."

Uncle Jacob grinned.

"There's no reason to hate—er—dislike either of them. They're both the laziest kind of mathematics. Look, I want you to try something—an experiment."

He paused for a moment and Albert waited.

"Do you ever play policeman, or pirates or anything like that?" Uncle Jacob asked.

"Sure."

"Well, try playing detective for a change. You're looking for a villain. You don't know whether he's a thief or a pickpocket. You don't even know his name. All you're sure of is that he's somewhere around and you've got to find him to keep him from doing any more harm. First thing you do is give him a name for your files. Right?"

Albert nodded, his eyes glistening with excitement.

"You call him 'X.'"

Again Albert nodded.

"Then you tail him. You follow him into one formula and out of it and into another or you slide down the hypotenuse of a triangle after him and chase him up the side wall of a parallelogram. Finally you catch up with him. You find out what he is and who he is. Now you've got him! You put the cuffs on him and take him in. That's all algebra is. Or geometry. Like to give it a try?"

"Yes," Albert said earnestly, "I would. I think that would help a lot."

Chapter 2

SHADOWS OF PREJUDICE

UNCLE JACOB's little game made a vast difference in Albert's work at school. As a matter of fact, it was responsible for much of his later success, for chasing the elusive "X" proved to have so great a fascination for him that mathematics soon became his favorite study. During the following year his marks improved amazingly, and he shot to the head of the class in algebra, geometry and physics.

Albert did not forget his promise to his parents. He never complained. But the hours spent in the classrooms of the Gymnasium seemed endless and, like the donkey whose master dangled a tempting morsel of new-mown hay just out of reach of his nose, Albert kept himself going from one class to the next by thinking of the fun that awaited him at home—books, talks, and his violin.

The wonderful evenings at the Einsteins' continued though a rival electrochemical shop *was* opened just across the street from the Einstein Shop, just as Albert's father had foreseen.

Business began to taper off. Some of their oldest and most faithful customers admitted that they were afraid not to take their trade to the new store. They had been told it was owned by someone very high in political and army circles whose influence could be of benefit to them in many ways.

Hermann and Jacob Einstein had done so well for so long that they had been able to set aside quite a sum of money. At first they were not too much concerned by the falling off of their profits. But as time passed and more and more of their customers deserted them, the partners knew something would have to be done before their savings disappeared. They began writing to friends and relatives in other cities and countries, asking if any of them knew of business opportunities.

Albert knew nothing of this, because his parents and Uncle Jacob were determined that their worries should not cast gloom over their cheerful evenings at home. So it came as a surprise when his parents told him that they were moving to Milan in Italy, where relatives had written to say there was a dry-goods and hardware store available.

It was even a greater shock to the boy when his parents told him that he could not go with them.

"You must finish your schooling so that you can get work, Albert," his father said. "I don't like to have the family separated and I don't like to think of you alone here in Munich, but there is no other way. You can stay at the Weills'. Their boy has gone into the army and they have a room. It will not be like staying with strangers."

"It will be for only a few months at a time," his mother added. "Your father will make enough money so that you will be able to spend the summer vacations with us."

"Of course," Albert said, smiling so that his mother would not cry. "I'll get along fine. It'll be fun being on my own."

He had promised that he would not complain about school and he meant to keep his word. But nobody was really fooled. It was a sad day for all of them when Albert and Mr. and Mrs. Weill saw his family off on the little train that was to take them on the first lap of their journey.

Determined to concentrate on his schoolwork so that he could finish the course as quickly as possible, Albert neglected his violin. With every possible minute spent on study, the days passed more quickly than he had dared hope. He had no time for loneliness or self-pity. He did not go to Milan during the summer vacation. Instead, he studied at home in order to get ahead of his class in the hope of being able to skip a year.

These were bad days for Albert. His many questions angered his teachers because they seemed to show that he knew more than they did. He couldn't be punished for this, but they were always on the lookout for ways of making him look silly in front of his classmates. Even this was not easy since, with his parents away and no friends or sports to distract him, there was nothing for him to do but study.

Perhaps that was why the teachers looked the other way and pretended not to hear when Albert's fellow students began making fun of him for being a Jew.

He had always known that his parents were Jewish, and that therefore he probably was too. But he had never thought about it very much or realized that it made him different from his fellow students.

His family, while deeply religious, were not followers of the orthodox faith. They did not believe in the vengeful God of the Old Testament, but in the freedom and dignity of the individual and in the right of every man, woman and child to worship God in whatever way he chooses.

He wished his parents were here so that he could ask them why the other boys and girls looked at him with such anger and bitterness. He wished he could ask them just what it meant to be a Jew. He couldn't ask the Weills. He could not think of an answer. This was not a case where he could call the unknown quantity "X" and seek its meaning in formulae.

He had promised his parents he would not complain, but this was different. He could feel the dislike of his classmates. They looked at him as if he had committed a crime. He would have to think of a way to get out of the Gymnasium and still have a chance of getting a diploma. He would keep his promise. He would not complain. And he would think of some means to be of help to his family; but he knew he would not continue in that school.

It was a dreary, depressing day. The rain, part sleet, slanted down on the windows of the train. There were five other passengers crowded into the stuffy compartment. There was every reason in the world why Albert should have been depressed, but he was not. To him the train might just as easily have been a golden chariot carrying him to the Royal Ball—or straight up into the clouds, for that matter. He was leaving Germany. Soon he would see his father and mother and Maja! He was going to Milan!

For the hundredth time he looked around anxiously to make sure he still had his belongings. His lunch and supper? Yes—there on the floor under his feet. His clothes? That bulgy brown-paper parcel crowded into the luggage rack overhead. His books? He hoped he'd have no trouble getting the round-topped leather trunk from the baggage compartment in the car's vestibule. He clutched his violin in its wooden case and leaned his head back against the seat. He was actually on his way to Milan!

As if he were reading about it in a book, he thought how this had been accomplished. It had been much simpler than he imagined once he had made up his mind to leave the school.

He had gone to the school physician and complained that he felt as if he were about to have violent fits. He said he often dreamed of choking his ancient-history professor. As he had expected, the doctor reported the interview to the principal, and Albert had been summoned to the principal's office.

He had been asked to wait in the anteroom. He had watched his teachers file in one after another to discuss his case with the principal. On the way out they had looked in his direction, some with pity, some in anger, but everyone with an expression of relief. When the principal had called him, his long face had been even more solemn than usual. He had told Albert that it had been decided to give him a certificate of ill-health; that it in no way reflected on his standing as a student but that it meant he would be dismissed from the school. He was free to go to any other school or even to return here if he could pass the physical examination. He was free!

He had hardly been able to keep from shouting it to the people on the streets. He had rushed to the Weills' house, and written his father at once asking for the fare to Milan. He had said he was feeling fine, so that they would not worry.

Mr. Einstein had sent the money and here he was! He was going to see his mother and father, and he felt no sense of guilt. He knew that no one would have taken his "symptoms" seriously unless they'd been as eager to get rid of him as he had been to leave, and they had jumped at the first possible excuse offered. He grinned to himself in the crowded railway carriage.

His family was overjoyed to see him. His mother exclaimed over and over again that he'd grown so tall she would not have recognized him. Maja too had grown and seemed surprisingly attractive to her big brother. His father and Uncle Jacob regarded him with undisguised pride. As a matter of fact, though he was unaware of it and would not have been interested in any case, he had grown into a very handsome boy with large dark eyes, brown wavy hair and a look of great strength.

One day he asked them why his fellow students had scorned him for being a Jew.

"We've often talked it over—your mother and Uncle Jacob and I," his father said. "We've wondered whether we should warn you about the way so many people feel about Jews."

"You see, Albert," his mother said, "people really don't know why they feel that way. Some hold our religion against us. Others dislike us as a race."

"We didn't tell you the whole truth in Munich, Albert," his father continued. "It *was* true that the army officers created competition to our store, but it was also true that our customers were told not to buy from us because we were Jews. That's why we came to Milan, where there is no prejudice against our people."

"It may be a good thing that this has happened when you are young, Albert," Uncle Jacob added. "It should teach you never to put labels on people because of their race, or the color of their skins. There are good people and bad people in every race. You must learn to judge each person for himself alone."

"In other words," Mrs. Einstein finished, "try to be a fine man no matter what race you happen to belong to. We don't think of Mendelssohn as a great Jew. We think of him as a great composer. By the way, how do you intend to be great? Have you any plans?"

"Yes," Albert answered unhesitantly. "I want to be a teacher."

"No more ideas of earning your living by playing the violin?" his father asked.

"I want to prove that you can help people to learn without punishing them," Albert said earnestly. "I want to try to get into the Polytechnic Institute in Zurich, Switzerland."

"But that's run by the Swiss Government and admits only Swiss citizens," his mother said.

"Then I will become one. I don't want to be a German any more. I don't believe it's right for a country to be run by soldiers and by force."

"Albert, you aren't old enough to be a citizen of any place." His mother spoke in laughter.

"Then I'll wait," Albert answered. "Or perhaps when they see how much I know about mathematics they will make some special arrangement for me to get into Polytechnic. Anyway, I'm going to try."

The last thing his parents wished was to shake Albert's self-confidence. They remembered only too well how shy he had been as a child, and they were glad to see that he was now ready to fight for what he believed in. So Mr. Einstein filled out the application for Albert to be allowed to take the entrance examinations to the great Polytechnic Institute which offered junior college courses, college courses and postgraduate work. To his surprise, his school record at the Munich Gymnasium won Albert the chance to take the exams.

Proudly the family dipped into their savings to send their boy to Switzerland where he took all the necessary examinations. A week later the self-confident young man learned that he had flunked in biology, zoology and all languages.

Chapter 3

PREPARATORY SCHOOL

UNLIKE his teachers at the Munich Gymnasium the professors at the Swiss Federal Polytechnic Institute in Zurich recognized in Albert the makings of a great mathematician or physicist. Instead of discouraging him from further attempts to enter the great university, they suggested that he go to a preparatory school in Aarau, Switzerland, for at least a year. There he would be able to make up his deficiencies. Their belief in him gave him new courage. His failure to pass the entrance examinations seemed to him a challenge rather than a defeat. He sent in his application to the school at Aarau without even waiting to write home for advice, and to his great satisfaction, his application was accepted.

He did not look forward to his term at Aarau with any pleasure, however. He fully expected to have to drill the dull rules of grammar into his head by endless repetition and grim determination. But he wrote home, packed his few belongings, and set out for the little village that backed up against the great Swiss Alps.

To his amazement, nothing was as he had expected it to be. On the contrary, the Aarau school gave Albert his first glimpse into what teaching could be like. He found complete freedom here. Students were enrolled at Aarau because they wanted to learn. The faculty was there to help those who needed it. The professors were not martinets. There was no feeling of military discipline. If someone wished to cut a class he cut it. No teacher rebuked him. But if he had difficulty in making up the lost classwork, no one sympathized with him; nor were the other, more conscientious students asked to suffer because of his absence. No lectures were repeated or reviewed. One attended class or had to make up the loss on one's own time.

There was a much closer relationship between teacher and pupil than Albert had dreamed could exist. He was amazed to find that he was welcome as a guest in many faculty homes. It was in this way that he came to know and love the delightful Winteller family.

Whenever Albert went to visit them, he was reminded vividly of those beloved evenings at home in Munich. The Winteller family loved music as much as the Einsteins did. When Karl and Hans and Maria and the professor and Mrs. Winteller learned that Albert played the violin, he was urged to bring it to their house. Thereafter, they spent many evenings playing chamber music or singing ballads and *Lieder*, and Albert forgot his homesickness and had a wonderful time.

His friendship with the Winteller family had many results. Mrs. Winteller saw to it, as his mother would have had she been there, that the tall, thin, growing boy got enough to eat.

Karl, a boy of his own age, became his first friend. Professor Winteller himself was so convinced that Albert had a great deal to offer the world of science and would make an excellent teacher that he wrote about him not only to Mrs. Einstein but to his own friends. It was as a result of these letters that he discovered that an acquaintance of his was a prosperous and distant relative of the Einsteins. This gentleman began sending a little money each month to help Albert pay for his living expenses.

Unknown to the kind professor, Albert, instead of using this money to pay for food, clothing and laundry, began to do without socks or hats or overcoats and to put aside as much as possible of this money toward the day when he would be old enough to become a Swiss citizen. He had learned that there was a registration fee that must accompany the application for citizenship, and he wanted to be sure that he would have enough money when the time came.

It seemed to Albert that he had barely settled down when the year was over. It was difficult to say good-by to the Wintellers who had become such close friends. In all likelihood he would not see any of them soon again, for if he could pass his examinations in the fall, he would be living at Zurich, at a considerable distance from Aarau. Only a week before this unhappy parting, Albert had an inspiration.

"Karl, why don't you come to Milan with me for the summer?" he exclaimed.

"That'd be great, Albert, but—perhaps I'd better let you try to persuade Father."

Albert was a convincing speaker, and Professor Winteller gave his consent to the plan.

In Milan, Albert was shocked to discover how thin and ill-looking his father had become. No one had written that Mr. Einstein's health had begun to fail, and that he could spend very little time in the shop. Nevertheless, in spite of their worries, the Einsteins all cheered up upon the arrival of the two boys. It soon became apparent, even to Albert who was not very observant of such matters, that Karl was much taken with his little sister, Maja. For a time the three young people went everywhere together. They went to museums and for walks around the beautiful city. They even managed, by waiting in line, to get standing room at the opera for a few lire.

It was a wonderful summer for Albert. He had never before had companions of his own age who liked the same things he liked. It was with real regret that he gradually came to realize that his sister and his friend did not always want him with them. When it finally dawned on him that they were in love, the summer was almost over.

One morning Karl went in to see Mr. Einstein alone. He told him he wanted to stay on in Milan and go into the Einstein business or at least help out at the store.

"It isn't only that I've fallen in love with your daughter, Mr. Einstein," he explained. "I have, and I do want to stay here in Milan to be near her. But I know we're both too young to be married for some time and that I must make money before I even ask her to become engaged."

"You seem to have thought of everything," Mr. Einstein said, stroking his mustache so as to hide a smile.

"There is something else. It's about Albert," Karl said.

"What's Albert got to do with it?"

"He's worried about the money it will cost for him to go to the Swiss Federal Polytechnic. He sees that the business needs more help. He knows that you are not too well. He doesn't want to create hardships for all of you by leaving and . . ."

"Did he tell you this?"

"No, Mr. Einstein. Albert is going to be a great man some day. My father thinks so. The dean at Aarau thought so."

"I think I know what you mean, Karl," Mr. Einstein said gravely. "I shall always remember something that happened when Albert was about five. He was just getting over the measles, and I used to bring him things to divert him. One day I happened to bring him a small compass. Nothing I had ever brought made so big a hit with him. He couldn't get enough of it. For months after he had recovered he carried it with him, asking questions of anyone who'd listen. What made the arrow move? What force was it that made it turn toward the north? What was magnetism? What was gravity? It was, as you just said, as if he was trying to understand the whole universe—at five!"

"You know, then, how important it is that he go to the Swiss Federal Polytechnic Institute—one of the greatest of its sort in the world?"

Mr. Einstein nodded. "I'll be proud to accept your offer to take his place here, Karl. It will be fine to have you with us. And I'm sure Maja will be delighted." Mr. Einstein smiled warmly on his prospective son-in-law.

Albert knew nothing of this. He only knew that the whole family escorted him to see him off when the time came for him to leave for Zurich, and that they all disguised the sorrow of parting by expressing the highest hopes for his success. They *knew* he would succeed.

Chapter 4

UNEMPLOYED SCIENTISTS

THE Swiss Federal Polytechnic Institute came as a revelation to the seventeen-year-old boy. If Albert was a young man without a country, so were many of the others registered at the great university.

There were refugees from Czarist Russia. There were students who had been deprived of the right to get an education in Hungary, in conquered Bavaria, and some from Poland and even some from France. From every part of Europe, freedom-loving people of all ages had come to this sanctuary where they could develop their abilities in their chosen fields.

Aarau had seemed like the home of freedom. How much more inspiring to Albert was this great campus, with its hundreds of Swiss and foreign students all working side by side.

From the beginning of his university career, Albert was seized by a desire to become "a citizen of the world." Here, where individuals from practically every European country were gathered together, patriotism or nationalism seemed out of place and ridiculous.

Now, for the first time, he began to regret that he had not tried harder at the Gymnasium to master more languages. He longed to discuss their mutual problems with his fellow students, and yet could not talk or understand their language.

It did not take long for him to realize that mathematics had a language of its own, a language that was understood by people who could not understand each other. The symbols of algebra, geometry, calculus, physics and chemistry were all that was needed to permit people of different languages to work out problems together.

It was this newly learned knowledge that brought about the crumbling of the wall he had always built between himself and strangers. He found that he was no longer shy with fellow students who, side by side with him, were seeking the basic truths of the universe.

During his four years at Swiss Federal Polytechnic, Albert made three very close friends. There was, first of all, Friedrich Adler, a blond boy who was even more bitter than Albert about the evils of militarism. He had seen his parents killed by a conquering German army, and he believed that nothing good could come of conquering by force. Since Albert had seen the disastrous results military discipline had brought about in Germany's public schools, he was a willing listener and soon became a firm believer in Friedrich's pacifist theories. Both boys decided they would never join the army to fight for any country, and they agreed that it seemed better to be shot as a traitor if their example could persuade others of the uselessness of trying to win arguments by force.

Marcel Grossman, who had been born in Switzerland, listened to Friedrich's impassioned arguments but disagreed with them. He believed that one should fight in defense of one's country. The other two boys conceded that Marcel had every right to his own beliefs and did not attempt to win him over. All three did their homework together and spent a great deal of their time in each other's company.

The fourth member of the group was a girl. Her name was Mileva Maritsch. From his very first meeting with her, at the table they shared in the physics lab, she fascinated Albert, because she was so completely unlike any girl he had ever met. She believed women should be educated. Most girls seemed to think that all they had to learn was how to cook and keep house for their future husband.

She spoke only Serbian of which Albert could understand not a word. And yet her eloquent eyes and long graceful hands enabled her to convey her meaning clearly in a sort of sign language of her own. Albert began studying Serbian, and Mileva got to work on unraveling the mysteries of German.

It was not long before she was able to explain to the three boys that she did not believe that girls should marry. The Emperor of Germany, Kaiser Wilhelm, had expressed the belief that women did not need to have an education or to know anything about politics or government. According to him, women should concentrate on the three K's—*Kueche, Kirche* and *Kinder,* which in English would be the three C's—Cooking, Church and Children. Mileva could not say enough about her scorn for this belief. She felt that women should be free to accept jobs and to work side by side with men. She believed in the equality of women long before it was stylish to hold such ideas. She wanted to learn enough physics and chemistry so that she could go back to Serbia and teach the poor people who could not afford an education.

As soon as Albert explained her views to the others, the three boys, greatly relieved, welcomed her as a companion. Now that they knew she had no silly romantic ideas about love-making or marriage, they were glad to discuss their classwork with her and seek her help in doing their homework.

All four members of this little group loved to take walks. They all liked music, and the beautiful old city of Zurich had much to offer them. Whenever their work schedule permitted, they enjoyed an evening of pleasure and relaxation.

Time sped by rapidly. Mr. Einstein sent money to Albert regularly. When Albert went home for his third summer vacation, he discovered why this had been possible. Karl Winteller had given the Einstein business the young blood and the drive it had lacked before. It was not making a fortune but there was enough money to support the whole family. Karl and Maja had waited for Albert to return and act as best man at their wedding, and he was overjoyed to see how happy the young couple were, and how well Karl fitted into the family. His father seemed even less robust than when Albert had last seen him, but he insisted that he had never felt better in his life. Mrs. Einstein was so happy that she seemed to have grown younger instead of older.

Perhaps seeing his sister and Karl so happy had something to do with what happened when he returned to school. It was the last thing in the world he would have guessed. He fell in love with Mileva. Even more surprising, in spite of all her ideas on the subject, she fell in love with Albert. They became engaged and began to make plans at once.

They agreed that they would be married just as soon after graduation as possible. They would both look for teaching jobs and with their fine record expected to get them easily. As soon as either one of them got a job they would be married.

Mileva could only get work in a private

school because she was a Serbian citizen but Albert had applied for citizenship four years before. By the autumn following graduation the five-year residence requirement would have been fulfilled so he could get a position in any one of the government-controlled schools—even the Swiss Federal Polytechnic itself.

Both Albert and Mileva worked harder than ever to improve their marks so that they could be graduated with high honors in physics, chemistry and mathematics in order to qualify for the best jobs available.

On graduation day, when they were handed their diplomas, Friedrich Adler and Albert Einstein were singled out for special mention. Albert was named the finest mathematician the university had ever graduated. But the next day when the four friends gathered in front of the bulletin board they soon learned that neither Albert nor Friedrich, in spite of their honorable mention, nor either of the others had been given a job.

They learned, too, that a vacancy on the faculty of the Swiss Federal Polytechnic had been filled by someone with a Swiss name. The four unemployed physicists turned and walked away in disconsolate silence. Three of them were angrier about Albert's situation than they were about their own.

"After all," Mileva said, breaking the long silence, "I am a woman. There has never been a woman professor in Switzerland. I can understand that they would hesitate. But Albert whom they called the greatest mathematician . . ."

"It's a great disappointment, Albert," Friedrich said, "but try to cheer up. There will be something soon. I'm sure of it."

"The trustees know nothing about my pending citizenship," Albert said mildly. "They may not have wanted to give this plum of a job to a foreigner. It may be that they think I've not had enough teaching experience."

"But you have!" Marcel exclaimed. "You're a great teacher. If it weren't for your tutoring I'd never have been able to get my diploma. And there are lots more like me."

"And have you told the faculty that, Marcel?" Albert asked. His eyes twinkled and he grinned at his angry friend. "Of course you didn't. And nobody else did either."

Chapter 5

"SHOEMAKER'S JOB"

"But what will you two do now?" Friedrich asked Albert and Mileva as the four of them sat at a table in one of the many attractive little restaurants that were patronized largely by students. "You can't get married without a job and there's no telling—"

"I'm going to stay right here, Friedrich," Albert said. "I think I'll be able to pick up some tutoring work for the summer school. Who knows, I may even be paid for it!"

Marcel and Friedrich both laughed.

"Not you," Marcel chuckled. "If somebody tells you a hard-luck story or shows you a hole in his socks you'll hand him back his tutoring fee to have his socks mended."

"I've heard there's a job open in Winterthur. I'm going there to see if I can't grab it," Friedrich said.

"Isn't that supposed to be a pretty tough school? Almost like a reformatory?" Marcel exclaimed.

"The tougher the better," Friedrich answered. "It'd give me a chance to test some of my ideas of teaching without resorting to beatings or any other form of physical punishment."

Marcel turned to Mileva. "What about the fourth member of the quartet? Staying here with your beau?"

They all turned to look at her, and Albert gave her hand a squeeze. He fully expected her to say she would wait and see what luck he had in his job hunting before making any plans. But she surprised him. She released her hand from his and spoke quickly.

"I'm going back to Serbia," she said. "If Albert can't get a teaching job here, I certainly can't. In my country the standards are not quite as high as here. The need for teachers is greater. And besides, I speak the language better than either German or French."

"But, Mileva," Albert protested. "We promised each other we'd get married as soon as just one of us has a job."

"Well? I am going to try. If I get one, we can get married."

All three of them stared at her in amazement.

"You mean you think Albert should come to Serbia to live?" Friedrich exclaimed incredulously. When she nodded he went on mercilessly, "You shouldn't even suggest such a thing. Albert is by far the most brilliant of us all. He has a great future. Would you want him to give it up and vegetate in some little far-off village?"

"Who says he would vegetate?" Mileva answered, her eyes flashing angrily. "Don't you all talk all the time about science being above nations—more important than the world itself? Does it matter so much where Albert does his figuring, his endless experiments, his constant reading?"

"But Albert will get a position of importance here soon," Friedrich said. "He can have access to the best labs, the best equipment. It will have a certain amount of prestige . . ."

"And you want me to forget about my own work and wait for him." Her eyes flashed. "Why should I! He's not willing to wait for me. Aren't you asking a lot?"

Albert looked at her. He had a strange premonition that marriage would not work out for two such ambitious people, but Mileva seemed very beautiful to him at that moment. Anger had brought color to her usually pale cheeks and her eyes seemed large and very moving. He reached out and took her hand again.

"You must do what you feel is right," he said gently. "Go back if that's what you want to do. I'll stay here and try my best to get a job. Give me a year, Mileva. That's all I ask—give me a year to make good."

The others were embarrassed. Someone changed the subject, and that was the way the matter rested.

Two weeks later, when Albert had still been

unable to find a teaching job, Friedrich came to him one evening.

"Albert, you know I've been engaged for the next term at the technical school in Winterthur. It's not quite as bad as Marcel claims. It's not like a reform school, but the boys do all come from poor families who want them to learn a technical skill by which they can earn a living. They're not likely to be interested in abstract science. But what I thought was this. If it would keep Mileva here, you could take my job at Winterthur for one semester, just as a temporary thing until something better comes along for you."

Albert was deeply moved. "Friedrich, I don't know what to say. No one has ever offered to do something so wonderful, but . . . I'll accept your offer, with all the gratitude in the world. Someday perhaps I'll be able to repay you. Do you think they will accept me as a substitute in Winterthur?"

"Accept you? When your credits are so much greater than mine? They'll jump at the chance."

He was right. The authorities at the Winterthur Academy were delighted to have him as a substitute, and Mileva agreed not to return to Serbia but to wait at least until Albert had taught for one full semester in the little "reform school."

From the very first day, his teaching there proved to be a difficult assignment. Often it taxed his patience almost to the breaking point. The boys had had a whole parade of new teachers. None had been able to maintain discipline. Albert got to the classroom a half hour before the class was scheduled to begin, and began writing a formula on the blackboard.

At eight-thirty the boys came in like a flood released by a broken dam, yelling, singing as they rushed for their seats. Albert remained with his back to them, apparently unperturbed, as he continued to write on the blackboard. He waited a few moments for them to settle down, but the noise continued. The boys shouted at each other, shot spitballs from rubber bands, and threw wadded paper all around the room. After what seemed like endless waiting, Albert turned around and held up his hand for silence. To his amazement the young roughnecks quieted down momentarily.

Albert stepped around the corner of the big desk and began.

"I am your new professor. My name is Einstein. I hope that we will–"

That was as far as he got.

"Einstein, Einstein, good old Einstein!" some of the boys began to chant in a rhythmic singsong. Others yelled other rude remarks.

Albert knew it would be useless to ask again for silence. He had sense enough to know that they were trying to make him lose his temper and that the louder he talked the more noise they would make. Instead of trying, he turned to the blackboard and began to write:

Those of you who do not wish to study under me can go home.

The boys gasped in amazement. Some of them started to their feet as if to leave the room, but others pulled them back into their seats. This was too good to be true. It was some kind of a trick. Those who left the room would probably be severely punished.

The noise faded. A few whispers were hushed. Albert turned from the blackboard to face them, and professor and pupils eyed each over warily like dogs who walk stiff-legged around each other before they decide whether they are enemies or friends. After a long moment, Albert, more than half expecting to be interrupted by whistles or catcalls, spoke quietly.

"Your parents have doubtless paid good money for you to be in this classroom so that you may learn things that will help you master a trade."

He paused. The silence remained unbroken.

"I am going to stay here because that is what I am being paid to do. But I can't teach you if you don't want to learn. So I meant what is written there behind me on the blackboard. Those of you who wish to can go home. You will not be punished by me. If you can explain it to your parents' satisfaction you need never report here again."

A minimum of whispers ran through the class but no one stood up. Knowing that a smile would serve to indicate to the boys that he was gloating over them, he remained solemn.

"There's one more thing," he said. "No matter what you do—any one or all of you—you will not be punished by force. There will be no whippings, no slaps with a ruler. I don't believe in that. I stood too much of it when I was in school."

There were no more whispers, just an attentive silence. After a moment he turned and, still with no smile or other sign of friendliness or what the boys would have called "softness," crossed to the blackboard.

"Today's lesson . . ." he began and proceeded to explain the formula he had previously written.

That was his first great victory, and it gave him confidence. There were outbursts from time to time. There was occasional insolence, but nothing as extreme as that first day had seemed to promise. At the end of the semester, parents and faculty alike felt that he had accomplished a near miracle. Whether they had really learned a great deal or not Albert was not sure, but he was certain of one thing. He had won the respect of his students.

During his term at Winterthur, Albert had written to every university in Switzerland and France applying for a job as instructor or assistant professor. When the job ended and

Friedrich Adler came to relieve him, he had received not even one nibble. Friedrich had done his best for Albert in Zurich but he, too, had to report failure.

"You've done a wonderful job here," his friend argued stubbornly. "Something will come along. It must. What are you going to do next?"

"Go back to Zurich, see Mileva, and try to persuade her to wait another six months."

"And if she refuses?"

"Then I will let her go to Serbia."

"Will you follow her if she succeeds in getting work?"

"Yes, I have promised."

Friedrich looked as if he wanted to say something—possibly to urge Albert not to do anything foolish, not to throw away the chance of a brilliant career—but he changed his mind. He knew that it was not wise to try to interfere with two people who were in love.

Mileva met Albert at the railroad station. The long separation had made them both realize how much they meant to each other. As he took her in his arms Albert hoped that nothing would ever separate them again. He wanted marriage and a home. He must find a job at once to make this possible.

Friedrich had reserved his old room in the boarding-house for Albert. When he left Mileva and went there to leave his bags and books, he found a letter awaiting him. It was from Marcel. Marcel had something to talk to him about. It was important.

And so it proved to be.

"It's a job," Marcel said several hours later as they sat with steins of good beer on the table between them. "But I'm ashamed to mention it to you."

"What do you mean, 'ashamed'?" Albert asked. "What kind of a job is it that you hesitate to name it? I've told you I must find a job—any kind of job—at once. I want to get married."

"But this is just a shoemaker's job."

"But that's fine!"

Albert had often heard the expression. It had been a favorite of his father's. A "shoemaker's job" was a bread-and-butter job—one that had no prestige, brought no glory, but paid enough to cover living expenses.

"That's the very thing I want, Marcel. Tell me what it is."

"Well—some members of my family are connected with the Swiss Government. I asked my uncle if he could help me find something for a friend of mine. I didn't tell him it was for Einstein who graduated from the university with top honors. I didn't want anyone to know that you haven't got the kind of position you should have . . ."

"*Please,* Marcel, out with it! Everybody pats me on the back and tells me I'm the greatest mathematician since Newton, if not actually

Copernicus, but nobody will give me a job. Now you actually have one for me, and I can't get you to tell me what it is!"

"It's in the patent office in Berne. It's checking inventions that people send in with their applications for patents. You have to see that there's no conflict—that no one else has patented the same idea already. That's all."

"It's wonderful! It's just what I've been hoping for. When can I start?"

"Right away, just as soon as—"

"I'll be married a week from Saturday. Then Friedrich can come from Winterthur to be best man and still get back for classes on Monday. You will give the bride away. Marcel, you're wonderful."

"I hope we're not making a mistake," Marcel said.

"Don't be so gloomy," Albert told him. "Of course we're not making a mistake. Let's go tell Mileva."

Chapter 6

WHAT IS RELATIVITY?

THE job in the patent office proved to be everything that Albert had hoped it would be. Checking on inventions—some of them daring and obviously intended to make life easier for people and some of them just crackpot ideas that could have no possible use—provided enough stimulus to hold his interest without making demands on his time after hours. He soon discovered that he could go back to thinking out the important problems that had tantalized him for so long. And he also learned that he gained a great deal by being able to discuss these projects with Mileva.

She, too, was happy and anxious to provide the companionship her husband seemed to need. During the first few months of their marriage, Mileva quite often expressed the intention of getting a teaching job or a position as a laboratory assistant. Before she actually got around to carrying out this idea, she learned that they were going to have a child. When their son, Hans Albert, was born, Mileva, in spite of her talk before marriage, became a careful and devoted mother. More than a year later, a second son, Edouard, was born to the Einsteins. Mileva found bringing up two healthy boys was a full-time job.

Although he dearly loved his sons, Albert at first missed his wife's companionship. This loss proved to be a blessing in disguise, for he turned more and more to the study of physics to fill in hours that would otherwise have been lonely.

More for his own amusement than with any serious purpose in mind, Albert began to write up some of the examples that seemed to disprove theories that had long been taken for granted. As he finished them, he submitted them to a publication called *Annalen der Physik,* or *Annals of Physics.* To his surprise, the first one was accepted by the editor, and it appeared in the following issue. Letters began to pour in to the publication from all over Europe. Some of these praised Albert as a man of vision and imagination. Most of them called him a radical and a crackpot. From that time on, Einstein's highly controversial articles appeared quite often in the *Annals.*

At first these articles were mainly concerned with seeming contradictions in fact. Regarding movement, for instance, Albert pointed out that to a man standing in a field watching a train go by, the train obviously was passing the telegraph poles that lined the track. But to a man on the train, the poles would seem to be passing the train, proving that motion is relative to the observer.

In an article concerning sound, Albert posed the following problem to his readers: When a man on a train travelling at sixty miles per hour blows a whistle, does the sound of the whistle travel 60 miles per hour faster than usual in the direction of the train and 60 miles per hour slower in the opposite direction? The answer was yes: to somebody *on the ground* the whistle's noise will travel at different speeds in these two directions. To the people *on the train,* however, the speed of the noise will be exactly the same as usual, because they themselves are moving with the whistle.

In reading of past experiments, Albert found something very puzzling. While everything else fitted into the above picture, the behavior of light was startlingly different.

Albert found that an experiment to test this question had been performed in 1887, by the American physicists Michelson and Morley. Try as they might, they could find no change in the speed of light even when the light source and observer were moving relative to one another. The speed of light, according to their measurements, is *not* relative—it is a constant of nature, always exactly the same no matter who is trying to determine it.

This result was very surprising to the scientific world, which in those days thought that light traveled through a mysterious *ether* somewhat as sound travels through air. The nonexistence of an ether means that some very curious things can happen. Albert returned to his man on the moving train. Suppose that he stands in the very center of the train. *To him,* light from a match would reach both ends of the train at the same instant. But to someone, standing on the ground, light from the match reaches the back of the train first, since it is "catching up" with the light, and only later on does it get to the front. Here is a case in which exactly the same thing appears very different indeed to different observers. and this peculiar effect could not be predicted.

Albert began his reasoning with two definite notions: The basic laws of physics are the same whether there is relative motion or not (things fall down on the train just as outside, objects have the same colors, and so on), and the speed of light (in vacuum, to be precise) is exactly the same to everybody, whether moving or not.

These two notions that Einstein adopted as the basis of his theory he called the Special Theory of Relativity.

One of the first things that appeared in the theory was the prediction that moving objects become shortened and heavier than they would be if they were not moving relative to an observer. In other words, if we were to throw a ball fast enough—almost, but not quite, 186,000 miles per second—it would appear flattened and would weigh more than it did to start with. When it comes to a stop, its original size and weight reappear. According to Einstein, the closer the speed of some body gets to the speed of light, the closer its length becomes to zero and its weight to infinity. If a body were ever to travel with the speed of light, it would have no size at all and an infinite mass, which is ridiculous; and so Einstein concluded that nothing could ever travel as fast as light or faster.

Even more astonishing was the result that even *time* is relative. Suppose we start out with two clocks, each exactly the same as the other. Now we shoot one of them off in a rocket ship at a high speed. The clock in the rocket will appear to be slow with respect to the clock left behind! If the speed of the rocket ship is, say, 160,000 miles per second, its clock will tick once for every two ticks of the clock left behind. To somebody on the rocket ship, though, his clock will seem to be ticking "slower" than he would be if he had stayed on the ground. If our rocketeer had left behind a twin brother, he would be younger than the twin when he returns to the earth after his voyage!

These amazing, almost unbelievable conclusions that young Albert Einstein was able to draw from his simple beginning were all eventually confirmed by experiments.

Still another conclusion of the Theory of Special Relativity has become the most famous of all. This is the fact that matter can be converted into energy, and energy into matter. We might take an atom of uranium, and cause it to break into two pieces in a laboratory experiment. When we do this, we find that the two pieces together weigh less than the original single uranium atom did—and that we now have a good deal of extra energy that we did not have before. The missing mass, m, has turned into an amount of energy E given by

$$E=mc^2,$$

where c is the velocity of light. Because c is so large, and c^2 that much larger, even a minute amount of mass is equivalent to an immense amount of energy. This is the basic principle behind the operation of nuclear reactors—such as the ones that power atomic submarines and ships—and atomic bombs. These devices get their enormous energies from the conversion of mass into energy when uranium atoms are split.

A closely related process takes place in the sun and other stars, where hydrogen atoms may be transformed, under conditions of great heat and pressure, into helium atoms. When this occurs, some mass is lost, and the resulting liberated energy causes the sun and stars to glow brightly.

Surprising as it may seem, the reverse process is also possible: Energy can be changed into matter. There are found in nature some very high energy light waves called *gamma rays,* exactly the same as ordinary light except that their frequencies are so high that we cannot see them. Gamma rays may be thought of as pure energy—they weigh nothing in the usual sense. When gamma rays pass near atoms, they often spontaneously turn into a pair of electrons, one with a positive electrical charge and the other with a negative electrical charge. And electrons most definitely *do* have mass. In this process, a gamma ray has *materialized* into a pair of electrons, with its energy having been turned into mass.

Amazing as the creation of the Special Theory of Relativity was, Albert Einstein—still in his twenties—had another bombshell for physics in 1905, the year in which the work on relativity was published. This was the theory of the *photoelectric effect,* in its own way as daring as relativity. In fact, Einstein received the 1921 Nobel Prize in Physics for his work on the photoelectric effect, rather than on relativity.

When light is shone on a metal surface, some electrons from the surface are emitted—they jump out. Curiously, the speed with which the electrons jump out depends upon the *color* of the light being used, and not on *how much* light there is. Blue light, experiments showed, produces faster electrons than red light.

Einstein's radical explanation was that the energy carried in a beam of light is divided into tiny separate bits, called *photons.* The energy of each photon depends upon the frequency of the light; in other words, upon its color. The photons of blue light, which has a high frequency, carry more energy than the photons of red light, which has a lower frequency. Thus when a photon of blue light happens to hit an electron in a metal, it can give it more energy than a photon of red light—which exactly explained the observations.

The concept that light has its energy in little packets is not at all easy to grasp. Thus his work was greeted with amazement and skepticism.

One day Albert walked into the office of the *Annalen der Physik*. He was, as usual, ushered in to see the editor.

"I have here a more than usually interesting article," Albert said. "It's about the possibility of releasing some of the energy that is imprisoned in certain masses of mineral matter."

"I'm really very sorry, Herr Einstein," the editor replied. "You're just too late. The articles for the next issue have all been approved and sent to the printer. There just isn't room for another article. Perhaps in two months . . ."

"I feel that it should be published as quickly as possible," Albert persisted. "It contains descriptions of experiments on mass energy and a formula that will enable man to measure the energy in any mass."

"Indeed," the editor said politely. "Well, well. But two months from now will do quite as well. It can't be so earth-shattering as all that."

"That's exactly what it is!" Albert explained. "If you won't publish it immediately I'll have it printed myself and distribute it to every university. Since you've been publishing all my less important articles, it would make your periodical look rather foolish."

"Very well, Einstein," the editor said quickly, "I'll pull one of the other articles and run yours."

However, instead of the vast explosion which Einstein had expected from the publication of his formula, $E=mc^2$, there resulted only the mildest of peeps. The ideas were just too great to be realized.

Chapter 7

ZURICH, PRAGUE, BERLIN

PERHAPS people weren't very much interested because they had a hard time understanding what the formula meant.

Once when he was lecturing in a hall in Berne, Albert began the lecture by saying, "I'm sure you will all find the theory very simple."

Such a roar of laughter greeted this remark that Albert could not continue for at least five minutes.

Almost no one believed in his theory, but Albert's confidence in it was in no way weakened.

"If my theory is successful," he said, "the Germans will claim I am a German and the Swiss will say I am a Swiss. But if it were to fail, the Swiss would say I was a German and the Germans would say I was a Jew."

Meanwhile things were happening among his family and friends that would affect his life in many ways.

In the first place, Mileva and he began to drift apart. She had given him great companionship in the days of their extreme poverty and loneliness. Now that the name Einstein was being discussed widely wherever physicists met, she began to remind him of the career that she had given up for him. They tried never to quarrel in front of the boys, but there was no longer any harmony between them.

Jacob Einstein died, and his brother, Albert's father, grew weaker and more feeble each day. Mrs. Einstein wrote Albert that she herself was too old to continue to nurse him and cook for him, so they had persuaded Cousin Elsa to come and live with them. ". . . You remember your Cousin Elsa—the one who wore braces on her teeth? She tells us that she always thought you would one day become a famous violinist. She has become a fine young woman. Your father is very fond of her. Oh, Albert lieber, I wish you could come home. I know that seeing you would do him good. He is so thin. He eats so little—even though he makes a big fuss over Elsa's cooking. I know it is not easy to make the trip but—if you can—please. *Soon.*"

But Albert could not leave Switzerland. Every day he went from one university to another seeking information about possible jobs. He planned to go to Milan just as soon as something definite had been decided about his future.

Marcel Grossman had given up all ideas of becoming either a teacher or a scientist and had gone into his father's business.

Friedrich Adler's ability as a teacher had

been recognized as a result of his work at Winterthur, and he was teaching at the University of Zurich as assistant professor. There was a chance of his soon becoming a full professor. He went to the directors and told them that while he was tremendously flattered. he thought they were making a mistake. With a man of Einstein's ability available, it would be wrong for them to select him. The Board explained to Friedrich that their rules demanded that before becoming a professor one had to become an assistant. The latter position was offered to Albert, and he accepted it gladly.

Feeling that his achievements had become recognized, he gave up his job at the patent office and took his family back to Zurich to live. But now, when at last things seemed very promising, he began having trouble at home. Mileva had been gallant and brave while the going was rough. Now that Albert was hailed as a success, she talked more and more of having given up her career to serve him and bring up his children.

Assistant professors were dependent for their salaries on the number of students in their classes. The Einstein theory was too difficult for most young men. Many were frightened away, and sought easier credits in other classes. This did not help the Einstein family's living conditions. Actually, Albert was making less money than he had as a clerk in the patent office.

Just when Albert was beginning to get discouraged, his theory began to receive more favorable attention. He was offered a full professorship at the University of Prague, in Czechoslovakia. Before he was allowed to teach, Albert had to be sworn in, and for this occasion he was required to buy a fancy uniform consisting of a long coat, black trousers with a red stripe down the side, a three-cornered hat and a sword.

At the university, Albert lectured about Isaac Newton to his classes. Gradually he became convinced that Newton's laws needed modification, particularly when they dealt with objects moving at speeds comparable to the speed of light.

Some of his essays on this subject attracted a great deal of attention. Less than a year later he was asked to come back to Zurich and serve as a full professor at his old university, the Swiss Federal Polytechnic Institute. For a young man in his very early thirties, this was a very great honor. He could hardly wait to write his parents.

He received a letter from his mother almost at once. She wrote to say that his father had just died, but that there had been time for her to read him the great news in Albert's letter. She wrote that their pride in him would help sustain her in her loneliness. Cousin Elsa was returning to Berlin, but Maja and Karl would continue to look after her.

On the last day of his stay in Prague, Albert's son Hans came to him with a question.

"Father, what is going to become of your beautiful uniform that you've worn only once?" he asked.

"Perhaps we can sell it," his father answered.

"Before you do, will you wear it just once more? Just once to please Edouard and me?"

"Why?"

"Because everybody talks about your clothes. We'd like to show them what you look like when you're dressed up."

Albert looked down at his son's earnest, upturned face and grinned.

"All right, Hans," he said. "What have I to lose? We're leaving town soon anyway. The worst that can happen is that people will mistake me for a Brazilian admiral."

So on their last day in Prague, Albert walked up and down the streets of the ancient city, with a little boy on either side of him and the great sword clanking at his belt, almost tripping him.

On his return to Zurich, Albert found himself flooded with invitations to lecture both on his theory of relativity and on his newer "field theory" of gravity. Encouraged by those offers he went more and more into the field of research physics. He felt now that this, rather than teaching, was the field he was best suited for. He did not like to have to limit classwork to the lectures prescribed by the university prospectus. He liked to discuss with his students all the wonderful possibilities for learning that he saw in the study of the universe.

It was at this time that he developed the theory that space is curved. This was the sort of theory that Albert loved to work on. Teaching seemed in many ways to be a waste of time. He was delighted, therefore, when he was visited in Zurich by a distinguished Austrian scientist whom he had met several years before. Max Planck came to Albert with the offer of not one, but three positions in Berlin.

One was a full professorship at the Academy of Sciences. This was the oldest and most outstanding of all scientific institutions. Full membership in it was limited to seventy. Its purpose was not teaching but research.

The second offer was to give a series of lectures on whatever subjects he chose as often or as seldom as he chose and to spend most of his time on research.

The third offer was from the Kaiser Wilhelm Institute. Here research was followed in several fields, but there was no separate institute for physics. Planck proposed that Albert should become director of the Physics Institute, as soon as it was organized. Till then he would act as consultant in other institutes of research.

Any one of these positions would have been flattering to a much older and more experienced physicist. Albert wanted very much to embrace Planck and thank him heartily for the offer, but he had to ask time to think it over. He remembered all too well the military discipline that had existed in Germany. He knew he would never be able to do his best work if those conditions still existed.

He pointed out to Professor Planck that he was now a citizen not of Germany but of Switzerland. If he could keep his Swiss citizenship he would jump at the chance to accept all three positions. Now it was Planck's turn to need time to think. He knew that Germany guarded its supremacy jealously, even in science. None of the boards of directors would like Einstein's demands. He would have to notify them. In the meantime, Albert hurried home to discuss the situation with Mileva.

She vetoed the whole idea. As a Serbian, she hated Germany and Germans.

"They're barbarians!" she exclaimed. "They think only of fighting and killing and conquering. Albert, do you want your sons to be drafted into the German Army?"

"I certainly do not!" he exclaimed, all his pacifist interest aroused. "But surely there's time for that later. They wouldn't be drafted when they're but children."

"Oh, wouldn't they? You've read that children are committed to four years' compulsory army service when they are eighteen. The truth is they're signed up from the age of four up."

"Then they will stay here with you," Albert said.

"Let us face things honestly, Albert. We have not been happy these last three years. If you will leave the children with me, I will give you a divorce. Then you can accept this great opportunity without endangering the lives of our sons."

"I think you are right, Mileva," Albert answered, "though I never would have suggested it. Of course," he added, "they haven't yet decided whether I may retain my Swiss citizenship, and unless they do, I shall not go."

Chapter 8

PROOF AT LAST

BECAUSE Kaiser Wilhelm II wanted to establish for Germany the reputation of having the greatest scientists, the finest artists and workers, in fact the best of everything, the German scientists were forced to give in to Albert Einstein's almost unheard-of demands. It proved fortunate for him that they did.

On his arrival in Berlin he lectured to a group of outstanding scientists. He was aware of the fact that most of them didn't believe in his theory that gravity bent light, he told them, but he was prepared to show them a way to test his theory.

He explained that when light passes near the sun, for example, it should be deflected by an amount which can be calculated. Therefore, when we see a star near the sun, it should appear slightly displaced from its normal position. But these stars are completely hidden from human sight, because the glare of the sun obscures them. Only when the sun is hidden, as during an eclipse, would one be able to measure the "displacement" of these stars, and even then only with very accurate instruments. The expected displacement would be equal to 1.75 seconds of an arc. This is a tiny portion of a circle, about as big as the diameter of a penny would appear to be if the penny were seen from a distance of two miles. There was to be a total eclipse of the sun in August, 1914, and this would be clearly visible from Russia. He therefore suggested that a group of scientists arrange to go to Russia on that date to view the eclipse.

Money was raised, expensive telescopes as well as cameras were purchased and packed, and the committee set out for Russia. The day they arrived at their destination, the First World War began. Russia joined forces with France and England against Germany. The Russians, not sharing Dr. Einstein's views about science being above all nationalistic borders, clapped all four of the German scientists in jail, where they remained till the end of the war. This, of course, was extremely hard on the four German scientists, but it also was hard on Albert, whose theory had to remain untested.

There was little doubt now that Albert held the three most important jobs any scientist could hold. His prestige was enormous. The Kaiser and his staff felt that it was necessary to combat the many stories of Germany's savagery by publicity about the great scientists and artists who made their home in Berlin. But Albert found it very lonely indeed. No one called him Albert any more. It was "Professor Einstein," or "Herr Professor Einstein" or "Herr Doktor Einstein." Albert began to wish for a few friends who would treat him with much less formality.

This was in his mind when he decided to look up his Cousin Elsa. He knew that she had married, that her husband had died leaving her with two daughters to bring up. He also remembered that his mother had always said that one day little Elsa would make a fine cook.

He was amazed to find her a charming, gracious, gray-haired woman with a delightful home. He liked her two small daughters, Margot and Ilse. When they asked him to bring his violin next time he came to visit, he knew that this, at last, would be a real home for him. It was not long before the once-famous "Einstein evenings" were resumed right in Berlin, in the center of war-torn Germany. As in the old days in Munich, everyone tried to get invitations to them. Soon Elsa and Albert decided to marry. The other members of the family were delighted, for they felt that Elsa would make a home for Albert in which he could relax after a day's hard work. He loved her cooking and was glad that she was not particularly interested in his work. He talked enough about his work during the day.

"My interest in mathematics," Elsa said laughing, "is confined strictly to the household accounts."

For the second time in his life Albert Einstein lived in an atmosphere that was in complete contrast to his surroundings.

Berlin was the very heart of the war. Infantry troops goose-stepped up and down the main avenues. Commands rang out at all hours of the day and night as guards were changed. There was a constant, almost deafening roar of the big guns aimed at far-off targets and there was the growl of the anti-aircraft batteries. Very infrequently there would be the wail of an air-raid siren. These were rare indeed, for the English had their hands full defending London against the German bombers, and the Americans had not yet entered the war as allies of the British and French. The Allies had too few planes to allow bombers to be risked on flights over the heavily defended German capital.

In the midst of the sounds, sights and smells of war, Albert Einstein and his wife Elsa lived quietly in their apartment. They spent evening after evening reading aloud from the works of Goethe, Heine and Schiller as Albert's father had once done in Munich so many years before. Albert Einstein was a citizen of Switzerland, and Switzerland was a neutral country that had refused to become involved in the world conflict. Thus, Albert could not be touched, even if there were some German patriots who felt that he should take a more active part in helping the German cause. He had only one answer to their criticism. He was a citizen of Switzerland. He had become a pacifist. He did not believe that might makes right. They must not ask him to take an active part in the war. He would do nothing against Germany but he would not fight for her cause. He wanted only to be left alone. But in spite of his determination and Elsa's best efforts to protect him, Albert's haven of isolation was invaded.

Late one night, in the winter of 1917, a bedraggled stranger presented himself at their door. Elsa, who had answered the doorbell, mistook him for a beggar.

"Wait here," she said, "I will go get you some—"

"I must see Dr. Einstein," the stranger said in a hoarse whisper. "Please, let me in. I must not be seen here in the hall. I may have been followed."

Frightened by the man's manner, Elsa tried to close the door but the stranger leaned his weight against it.

"No!" Elsa exclaimed. "You must not—"

"What is it, *Liebchen?*" Albert called out from the study.

The stranger gave Elsa no time to reply.

"Mrs. Adler sent me," he called out. "Dr. Einstein, you must listen! I've come a long way. I've come to ask your help."

Again Elsa tried to block the doorway, but by this time Albert had come up behind her.

"Adler?" he said musingly, "I know no Mrs. Adler."

"You know her husband. Friedrich Adler."

"Friedrich!" Albert exclaimed, and moved toward the stranger. "This may be a trick. He may be armed!" Elsa cried out and tried to remain between the two men.

"I *am* armed," the stranger said. He withdrew a revolver from his inside coat pocket. Elsa screamed, but the man swung the revolver around in his hand and offered it, butt first, to Albert. "Take it," he said, "but for God's sake, let me in!"

Albert pushed the gun aside and, grasping the man's forearm, ushered him into the living room. Elsa closed the front door and followed.

"Where is Friedrich Adler?" Albert asked. "I've not heard from him for a long time."

"He is in prison," the stranger said. "He has been sentenced to be shot by a firing squad just ten days from tomorrow's dawn. That's why I'm here. You are the only one who can help."

Again Elsa tried to warn Albert of a possible trap, but the visitor anticipated her thoughts.

"I'm Friedrich's brother-in-law," he said. "We used to talk of you all the time. Friedrich told us of your achievement in discipline when you took his place at Winterthur. He has often spoken of your first wife Mileva and how he had tried to advise you not to marry her."

"Enough," Albert interrupted. "I know that you are no impostor. Why was Friedrich put in prison?"

"He killed a man."

"Friedrich! I can't believe it!" Albert exclaimed. "He was always so kind—so gentle!"

"He shot and killed Count Turckh, Austria's Prime Minister, because Friedrich believed him to be responsible for the start of the war. He has admitted it. He will not claim any justification other than that. He says 'Of course I knew what I was doing. The man deserved to die.' "

Albert looked at his wife.

"What can you do, Albert?" she asked.

"I don't know. But Friedrich did more for me than any living man. I must do whatever I can."

It turned out that there was a great deal that Albert Einstein could do. He did what he would never have considered doing in his own behalf. He pleaded with the Kaiser for a retrial and begged to have Adler considered a prisoner of war instead of a murderer. His request was granted but the terms were steep. Adler was transferred to a military prison, retried, and given a sentence of eighteen years' imprisonment. And Albert Einstein became a citizen of Germany. Now that beleaguered but still arrogant country could boast that the greatest scientist since Copernicus was a representative of German "Kultur."

Later, when Adler had served most of his sentence and an arrogant little paper-hanger assumed charge of Germany's policies, it meant that there would be a price on the head of

Albert Einstein. But even had he known that at the time, Albert Einstein would not have hesitated to discharge what he considered a debt of honor.

In 1917, while the war was still going full blast with indications that German military might and know-how might well prove superior to the combined armed forces of England, France and Russia, there was a man in London who lived in utter scorn of the daily bombings of some of London's most beautiful old buildings, and the tragic loss of English lives. Like Albert Einstein in Berlin, this man considered that scientific truth was of far greater importance than the conquering of one nation by another. This man was the Astronomer Royal of England.

Ignoring falling debris and wailing air-raid warnings, he attended a meeting to which he had summoned a small group of equally devoted scientists. He reminded them that a scientist named Einstein had suggested three years before that light was bent by the sun's gravitational pull, and that the only way this theory could be proved was by photography. The stars nearest the sun could be photographed at the time of a total eclipse of the sun. Such an eclipse, he said, was scheduled to take place two years hence, in 1919. At that time the obscured sun would be completely surrounded by a group of very bright stars, the Hyades. There were two places from either or both of which the eclipse could be best observed and photographed. One was a place in Northern Brazil in South America; the other was an island in the Gulf of Guinea, in West Africa. His listeners grew very excited. They must send expeditions to both places to test Einstein's theory of gravitation.

No one expressed the natural doubt that these expeditions would be able to get past the German U-boats surrounding England. No one pointed out that England had been asked time and again to tighten its belt another notch because food was scarce and money practically nonexistent. These men were scientists living in a world of their own, far removed from war and the everyday problems of everyday people. They decided to raise the money to send out the two expeditions so that photographs could be taken and observations made from both vantage points. In this way if one expedition met with bad weather in which the stars were not visible, the other expedition might have better luck.

The Royal Society and the Royal Astronomical Society of England went about the business of raising the very large sum of money needed to finance these two expeditions. Unbelievably, they actually succeeded in raising this money and in purchasing the finest available telescopes and photographic equipment, still with no idea of how the parties were to get out of England in wartime with London under heavy daily bombardment.

Suddenly, in November 1918, Germany was defeated. The war was over! Calmly, the two British expeditions set out early the following year. One, headed by Sir Arthur Eddington, a noted English astronomer, headed for the island of Principe in the Gulf of Guinea, the other for Sobral in Northern Brazil.

Both groups were successful in obtaining photographs. Whether or not these would prove or disprove Albert's theory that light was bent by 1.75 seconds of an arc out of its course could not be told until the photographs were compared with some taken in London at a time when the Hyades' distance from the sun was much greater. Then these stars would no longer be exposed to the sun's gravitational power.

Months passed. The photographs were studied. Astronomers discussed all possible errors and interpretation. Then, on a day in November 1919, the scientists, mathematicians and astronomers met by invitation in the chambers of the Royal Astronomical Society, and to a spellbound audience the Royal Astronomer announced that the photographic plates had completely verified Einstein's prediction made more than six years before. The rays of light were bent as they passed close to the sun. They moved out of their course by 1.64 seconds of an arc, instead of the 1.75 seconds predicted by the great Swiss scientist with only pencil and paper as his instruments. For the first time in two hundred years the findings of Isaac Newton had been challenged and had been found to need modification.

Sir J. J. Thomson, president of the Royal Society, described Einstein's theory of relativity as "one of the greatest achievements in the history of human thought. It is the greatest discovery in connection with gravitation since first Newton enunciated his principles."

Headlines that said, in large black type, REVOLUTION IN SCIENCE, NEWTONIAN PRINCIPLES OVERTHROWN! normally would have attracted a great deal of attention. But these particular words happened to appear on the first Armistice Day—the anniversary of the end of World War I—and more readers were interested in looking at pictures of the ceremony at the tomb of the Unknown Soldier or in reading so-called "human interest" stories than in headlines that seemed to refer to something of interest only to scientists. No one in England had any idea, that November 7th, 1919, that those headlines would have a great meaning in another war more than twenty years later.

But things were quite different in Berlin. There, naturally, there was no reason to celebrate the anniversary of Germany's final defeat, so the triumph of Albert Einstein was a cause for great joy. Reporters rushed to the apartment of the Einsteins where Albert was discovered playing the violin for his wife and two small adopted daughters. The little scientist was shown copies of Sir Thomson's speech as well as copies of the eclipse photographs. He realized that all the doubts that had been cast upon his theory, all the challenges to his integrity—all of these had been wiped out in one moment. He realized what this would mean to him and to his family. He could say nothing. He looked again and again at the photographs that had been handed him. "Wonderful!" he exclaimed. "What wonderful, wonderful pictures!"

Albert and Elsa found themselves suddenly swamped in a tide of visitors. Some were scientists who came offering positions in other countries, some were celebrity hunters who wanted the Einsteins to come to dinner so they could show them off to their friends. Some were inventors with strange ideas. Some were portrait painters, reporters, magazine writers, photographers. To Albert, who was always shy and self-effacing, it was torture. Elsa then took over. She decided that the family would be better off if they moved into a house outside of Berlin. She found a delightful cottage on the shores of a lake at Caputh, some twenty miles out of town.

The move did not discourage the long line of visitors. Strangers tramped through their lovely garden and even tapped on their windowpanes. Elsa made herself responsible for protecting her husband from those who were merely celebrity hunters.

He continued his teaching at the three universities. In fact he did more teaching and less experimentation than he had originally planned. He seemed to be a contented man and yet there were moments when Elsa thought he was worried. However, she was completely unprepared for a scene which took place one day in the spring. She was in front of the house using the pruning shears on the privet hedges lining the approach. At the same time she was keeping an eye on her wrist watch, to make sure that the young inventor she had sent back into the garden to see her husband would not overstay the time allowed him.

Suddenly she heard Albert's voice raised in anger.

"Get out!" he was shouting. "I want to hear no more about it! Get out!"

Albert never raised his voice! He believed that only people who didn't know what they were talking about used loud voices and that they did so to hide their lack of knowledge. What could be wrong? Elsa dropped the shears as her husband and the young man appeared from around the back of the house. The postman and some children and older visitors were coming up the walk, so she was amazed to hear Albert continue his shouting without regard to anyone.

"Don't argue with me. Don't try to tell me

what can and what cannot be done! I tell you no one will ever use my formula to make an explosive. It cannot be done!"

The young man with him surprisingly refused to be cowed but continued expostulating and waving his hands. Only bits of what he said could be heard because of Albert's vehement denials.

"I've only taken your formula as a springboard. . . . It's all right here. . . . If you'd only look at it. It's a natural outgrowth of $E = mc^2$."

"No!" Albert shouted. "It is not! No one will ever release the energy locked in the atom. It's purely theoretical—"

By this time both men had reached the walk, and Elsa hurried toward them.

"What is it, Albert? What's wrong?" she asked.

"Nothing's wrong, *Liebchen,*" he answered soothingly, but it was obvious that he was very much upset. She turned to the young man who looked completely bewildered.

"You'd better leave," she said. He nodded and, still shaking his head as though trying to figure out what he had done to arouse the great scientist's anger, he walked down the path. Albert looked after him, the flush fading slowly from his cheeks as the newly arrived visitors waited politely to be greeted. He did not even notice them. For a moment Albert looked at his wife.

"He wanted my help in developing a bomb

that would destroy the world," he said. Without saying any more he went inside, leaving Elsa to ask the new arrivals to wait patiently for a little while.

This strange little episode was never referred to again by anyone, although in later years Elsa had occasion to think of it many times. She found it strangely disturbing, for it seemed to indicate that her husband was under some kind of secret strain which he was not sharing with her or anyone else. From this time on she noticed that he wanted to do less experimentation. He did not talk much about his famous formula but became more and more eager to apply some of the truths he had learned to other fields. To the world in general there was nothing strange about this. But to Elsa who loved him and knew him so well, it seemed as if he were trying to avoid a discovery that would be too dangerous to handle.

Chapter 9

AROUND THE WORLD

SHORTLY after the world-wide acceptance of his theory of relativity—between the end of 1919 and the spring of 1920—Albert began to change. His wife Elsa, in whose eyes he could do no wrong, was the first to notice it. Very few others did, because the change was gradual.

Possibly it was brought about by the premonition that through his formula atomic energy might be released before the world was prepared for it. He dreaded this awful power, this tremendous capacity for destruction which waited to be unleashed. Although as a scientist it was his duty to go on exploring the possibilities of atomic power, he felt that as a civilized man who despised militarism and longed for permanent peace for the world he should carry his atomic studies no further. As a scientist he had to admit that there was energy in certain kinds of matter—possibly in every kind of matter—and that it could possibly be released. But he refused to help in actual experiments, abandoned his own laboratory work, and turned more and more toward other matters. These matters, to everyone's surprise, included politics, government, and the increase of tolerance throughout the world.

The Kaiser had gone into exile. Germany, now a republic, faced the tremendous task of reconstruction. Just as soon as the victorious Allies could succeed in rebuilding her shattered cities and help to establish sound means of doing business, Albert's fatherland would again take its place as one of the great countries of the world. Albert thought he could help toward this goal by showing confidence in the new regime, and he applied for German citizenship. Fortunately for himself and for his family, however, he did not renounce his citizenship in Switzerland.

Things did not develop as the freedom-loving countries hoped they would. Times were bad, money was scarce and it was easy for those who wished to stir up trouble to find audiences that would listen to their complaints.

It was at this time, when Germany was in the throes of postwar depression, that ex-Corporal Hitler began to address crowds wherever he could find them, and tell them that all Germany's troubles began with the foreigners and Jews. Little by little he built up a feeling of uneasiness. Albert was reminded of his high-school days in Munich, when he had felt his fellow students' eyes turned toward him with hate-filled looks.

But this time Albert was in a position to voice his anger and resentment. When fellow scientists, jealous of his success, began referring to his theory of relativity as "Jewish mathematics," his usually mild temper boiled over. Palestine and many cities in the Egyptian desert had been freed from Turkish rule when it was captured by the British in the recent war. Many of the persecuted Jews in a great many different countries began to think of the possibility of going to Palestine to live and creating there a nation made up of Jews from all over the world. Those who were interested in this plan called themselves Zionists. As Albert became more and more aware of the insults and indignities that were being heaped on Jews in Germany, and the increased difficulties of their being able to obtain an education or technical training for their children, he became more enthusiastic about the idea of a return to Jerusalem. He thought that Jews should throw off the yoke of prejudice and persecution and establish their own nation in the country mentioned in the Bible as the home of the Jews. So Albert Einstein, who had always believed that science, physics, mathematics and philosophy were international, stronger and more important than any love for one's own country, now, in his early forties, began to urge a nation for the Jews.

Word of Albert's feelings reached a famous English chemist, Dr. Chaim Weizmann, who had been asked to act as leader of the newly organized Zionists. Dr. Weizmann made a special trip to Berlin to see Albert Einstein, one of the most famous Jews in the world at that time. Dr. Weizmann asked Albert if he would be willing to use his influence to help raise large sums of money for the development of Palestine, and especially for schools, colleges and universities that could compare with the best anywhere. Albert agreed to do anything he could to help.

Mr. Weizmann persuaded Albert to make a visit to America in the spring, to help arouse interest and raise money for the Hebrew Institute in Jerusalem. In the meantime, however, the Professor's reputation was growing day by day. He was invited to go to the University of Leyden in Holland to deliver a series of lectures. His first lecture drew an audience of fourteen hundred eager students of all ages. Albert could not help but think back to the time when, as an assistant professor in Zurich, he had been paid at the rate of so much per student, and his first lecture had been attended by only two.

He and Elsa enjoyed the many beauties of Holland and the Dutch Lowlands, and he was glad when the university asked him to stay on for a whole series of lectures.

From Holland they went to Prague. Albert could not resist the opportunity to return to the city which he had loved, though he had not been too successful financially—the city where he had donned the "Brazilian admiral's uniform" to please his two small sons. After one of his most successful lectures in Prague, he and Elsa were in a small room adjoining the lecture platform, receiving the congratulations of the members of the audience who chose to come backstage to meet the speaker. Albert's eyes opened wide in surprise when he saw two tall, nice-looking boys standing in line waiting to greet him. They were his sons, Hans Albert and Edouard. He was delighted to see them and to have them meet Elsa. Afterward the whole family went to a little café, and the boys told the Einsteins that their mother, Mileva, had wanted them to come to hear their father lecture. Judging from the way they spoke of their life at home, Mileva had brought them up without bitterness toward Albert and Elsa, and they felt grateful to her for what she had done.

Hans Albert told his father that he, too, wanted to become a physicist someday. Albert assured him he would give him a helping hand.

"I don't think I want to get help just because I'm your son, Father," the boy said. "I want to make good on my own—or not at all."

Albert patted his arm affectionately. He felt very proud of his son and knew that the best way to help him was to let him work things out for himself.

Edouard presented no such problem. He wanted to be a doctor when he grew up.

"Your mother," Elsa asked. "Is she well?"

"Oh very well!" Edouard replied. "She says

she enjoys her work so much that the days pass very quickly."

"Her work?"

"She teaches at the university three days a week."

"I'm glad," Albert answered. "I am very happy for her."

Later that night a reception was held in the ballroom of the largest hotel in Prague. Albert was the guest of honor. He invited his sons to attend the gala occasion. At the height of the festivities he was called upon to make a speech.

"I don't think anyone here really wants to hear me make a speech or deliver a lecture on my theory of relativity," he answered from the small platform that had been built at the end of the ballroom. "So, instead of making a speech, I'm going to play the violin for you."

He played Mozart and Bach. The audience loved his playing and applauded and shouted until he consented to do an encore. Both Hans and Edouard remembered that their father played, but neither had any idea that he was quite a performer and they were both surprised and very proud.

Albert now gave a series of lectures in Austria and Hungary, where the aftereffects of the war were still heartbreakingly obvious. Then, with the greatest interest and enthusiasm for his first sight of the New World, Albert and Elsa left Europe, as he had agreed to do, to talk in behalf of Jerusalem for the Jewish people in America.

Many scientists felt that Albert Einstein was making a grave mistake in allowing himself to stray from the field of science to a project involving human relations.

"In this great movement," Einstein said to reporters who awaited him eagerly at the dock in New York, "it is not enough that we act as individuals. The time has come for us to tackle tasks which only nations as a whole can perform."

"Dr. Einstein, did you not often speak out against nationalism as opposed to science which should know no national limits?" one reporter asked.

Albert Einstein shook his head impatiently. "If we did not have to live among intolerant, narrow-minded and violent peoples, I should again be the first to ask for the overthrow of all nationalism," he answered.

On this visit he was tremendously impressed by the absence of fear and the freedom to study all subjects with no restrictions. Both he and Elsa were as thrilled by the sight of American democracy in practice as young Albert had been at Aarau, in Switzerland, where he had his first glimpse of studies not enforced by cruel discipline.

The Einsteins and Chaim Weizmann traveled from the Atlantic to the Pacific, meeting people, speaking and lecturing on behalf of the new university in Palestine. There were several notable results. They succeeded in raising over a million dollars. They came to admire and respect the American way of life, and they returned to Germany impatient with the needless restrictions, formalities and hardships that were imposed on scientists there.

On his return to Berlin Albert was approached by some of the young men who were rapidly becoming powerful in Germany. He was asked to sign a paper approving of the "German Militaristic Spirit of Conquest." To his disgust he saw the names of several well-known scientists and inventors already listed.

"I'd rather be torn to shreds than participate in such doings!" he exclaimed and became more adamantly pacifistic than ever before.

An organization known as the Commission for the Co-operation of Intellectuals was formed, and Albert Einstein was invited to join with scientists, writers and other creative people from every nation to work together for world peace.

As a result of his feelings against war, he now began to receive invitations to lecture on pacifism as well as on scientific subjects directly related to his theory of relativity. Since he was most reluctant to develop or help to develop the destructive possibilities of the released power of the atom, he gladly accepted these invitations. In addition, such tours promised to give both him and Elsa a chance to travel to parts of the world that they might never have seen.

England was still bitterly resentful of the Germans, yet Albert Einstein was formally welcomed by the Royal Society of Astronomers which had been responsible for the confirmation of his theory. He won the respect and affection of the general public by visiting the tomb of the Unknown Soldier.

It was the same everywhere. In France there was even more bitterness against the Germans than in England, but Einstein's simplicity and obvious sincerity in his desire for world peace won him friends and followers everywhere he went.

Discontent was growing in Germany as a result of a severe economic depression. Like the growl of distant thunder, there were mutterings among the people. They were dissatisfied with the way democracy was working out for them. They had been given orders for too long. They were unable, as yet, to think and plan for themselves. They were, without knowing it, making themselves the material of which mobs are made—mobs that can be influenced by anyone who shouts loud enough and often enough.

But in Japan, in China, in Asia, Einstein was the man of the hour. He was a German who did not want to brag or shout or bully. He was simple and modest and kind and the peoples of the East loved him as they had loved no Westerner before him.

In 1921 Albert Einstein suddenly and unexpectedly found himself the recipient of the Nobel Prize in physics for scientific achievement. The award, however, was not made for the theory of relativity. There was still too much controversy on this subject. The Swedish Academy of Sciences avoided having to take a definite stand on relativity by awarding the prize for Einstein's discovery in 1905 of the photoelectric effect, and his work in the field of theoretical physics. It carefully stated that the award, which included a payment of $50,000 in cash, was made in recognition of the great contribution he had made toward relating science to the betterment of world conditions.

He had been concerned and hurt by the many criticisms heaped upon his graying head by those who said that a scientist should not allow his interest to be diverted but should concentrate on study. There had been a great many former friends who had not hesitated to tell him that "a shoemaker should stick to his last." The Nobel Prize was a complete answer to those critics. Gaily and with the hearty approval of Elsa, he sent half of the money to his first wife, Mileva. He wrote that this was in appreciation for her help and loyalty and love when times had been bad. Then, in defiance of his critics, he helped to organize the "War Resisters International" and wrote an urgent appeal to the newspapers.

"I appeal to all," he wrote, "to declare that

they will refuse to give any further assistance to war or the preparation of war. I ask them to tell their governments this in writing and to register this decision by informing me that they have done so."

Chapter 10

DANGER

THE shadow of war, however, was not far off. Adolf Hitler, young, power-hungry, had become leader of the National Socialists, and then Chancellor of Germany. In an incredibly short time, Hitler, *der Führer,* had all Germany under his thumb.

According to the philosopher Hegel, all nature operates on a theory of the survival of the fittest. Weak things die, or are killed by the strong. Only those most fit for life survive, and in this way the species improves itself. Hegel believed that the same could be done with man. The strongest, handsomest and most intelligent should continue the race. This *Übermensch,* or "Superman," Hegel said, was the Aryan: the tall, blond, blue-eyed Germanic type.

When Hitler came to power, he put Hegelian philosophy into effect. The result was a terrible persecution of all non-Aryans, and the first to fall victim to this were the Jews.

Dr. Albert Einstein, discoverer of tremendously important universal truths, hailed everywhere—from the West to the farthermost part of the Orient—as a citizen of the world, was a Jew. He was also a liberal and apparently completely without fear, for he said in an interview: "Let every man be respected as an individual and no man idolized." This was hardly the kind of remark likely to endear the speaker to the conceited, power-hungry young Hitler. It became obvious that Einstein must be got rid of.

It was late one afternoon in midsummer that Elsa saw the man with the pistol. She had been pulling dandelions from the lawn. Albert, she knew, was in the little room she'd had built onto the house to serve him as a study. A shadow fell across the lawn and she looked up just in time to see a man, crouching as he ran, turn the corner of the house toward Albert's study. As he turned, the sunlight glinted for a moment on the long blue-steel barrel of a German Luger pistol. Instantly and instinctively she knew that this man meant to kill her husband. Without a second's hesitation she was up from her knees and running, clutching the trowel as if it were a dagger. She did not follow the man. She ran to the opposite side of the house, for she knew that that way lay her only hope of reaching the study before the assassin could make it.

Rounding the corner, she was just in time to see the man as he peered into the window of Albert's study. He started to raise the pistol. Elsa screamed and threw the trowel. It missed the man's head but crashed into the study window and had the effect of startling the man and alerting Albert. Elsa rushed toward the man and jumped at him before he had time to recover from his surprise. Albert ran out through the broken French windows and grabbed the pistol out of the man's hand.

Later, when the police arrived, he broke down and confessed that he was trying to kill Albert because there was a prize of $5,000 being offered to anyone who would assassinate the world-honored scientist. After the police had taken the man away, Elsa felt weak in the knees and had to sit down. Her husband looked at her with great affection. He knew her well, and was sure that if he thanked her for saving his life or praised her for her bravery, she would probably burst into tears. Instead, he tried to treat the whole affair lightly and to make a joke of it.

"Look at this head of mine!" he exclaimed, pointing at his wind-blown gray hair. "Just look at it, Elsa! Think of it! There's a price of $5,000 on it just as it is—and you thought I ought to get a haircut!"

The tough little scientist had never been one to be affected much by threats. They acted upon him as a challenge. He was tempted to stay on at their delightful house at Caputh but when a second attempt was made on his life, this time blocked by the gardener, he decided that it was not fair to endanger not only his own life but those of his loved ones because of his own stubborn pride.

He accepted temporary sanctuary in Belgium. There he began planning for a world lecture tour. Reluctantly he decided to resign from the Academy of Science and from the Kaiser Wilhelm Institute. He felt that it might be best for his friends and colleagues, many of whom were not Jewish, if he were to offer them an easy and graceful way of breaking their connection with him.

To his surprise, his resignation was accepted quite without regret, and he was accused of disloyalty and even of communism. In fact, it was at this time that the words "bolshevism" and "communism" were first used in connection with his name. He read with mixed feelings the report of a national woman's club in the United States which declared him definitely "communistic" in his teachings. It was possibly this as much as any other single thing that influenced him to accept three terms of teaching at the California Institute of Technology at Pasadena.

This gave him a welcome opportunity to renew acquaintance with old friends of his, such as Professor Albert Michelson whose experiments in the measurement of the speed of light had stimulated young Albert's imagination, and the famous physicist Millikan, who had also been an inspiration to the young struggling scientist in a lonely world of new ideas.

Another old friend was Dr. Abraham Flexner,

well known in America as a daring and liberal educator. He urged Albert to join the teaching staff of the newly founded Institute for Advanced Study at Princeton, N. J. This sounded like the sort of job he'd looked forward to all his life. He allowed Elsa to settle the matter of salary, "so she won't complain that I don't allow her enough for household expenses." He never did ask what the final figure was.

They moved into a lovely house with a great deep garden on Mercer Street in Princeton. The academy was not a part of the university campus, but one could reach it by walking between the campus buildings if one wished.

Here the Einsteins settled down in complete happiness. War and hatred might fill the world but here there was a little island of peace. Margot and Ilse joined the Einsteins as did Albert's sister Maja, his loyal secretary Helen Dukas, and their newly acquired terrier, Chico.

He often wondered how the rumor that he was a communist sympathizer had begun, and was curious enough to make a point of asking one of the members of the national woman's club when he met her at a faculty function, several years after his family had become accepted as a beloved part of the Princeton scene.

"In a lecture you made at a liberal arts college in 1933," the lady explained, "you said that you had come to the conclusion that there was no absolute truth in mathematics, and as this was the most precise of all sciences, you did not see how there could be such a thing as an absolute truth in philosophy or politics or in religion."

"I recall saying something of the sort," Einstein admitted. "But please continue, for I must confess that I fail to see—" The lady looked at him reprovingly.

"You then went on to say that you could understand how to the unprivileged rural peasant of Russia, the system of free enterprise might prove less satisfactory than simply being issued orders by a paternalistic government. In short, that communism might mean one thing to a Russian and quite another to an already freed individual in a free society like the United States."

"Madam," Albert Einstein asked with amused irony, "do you still consider that to be a pro-communist statement?"

"Well—"

"Let me put your mind at rest, madam," Albert continued, his eyes twinkling. "My stepdaughter Margot, my secretary Miss Dukas, and I have just had the honor to be accepted as citizens of the United States. I don't want you to lose sleep worrying lest we plan some violent act against the government. I still think everything—including a point of view—is relative. But—"

He leaned closer to the startled lady and whispered melodramatically.

"From our viewpoint here at Princeton—we like it here!"

During those early years at Princeton, Albert Einstein found himself in a strange position. His theory of relativity was generally accepted as being true yet everyone agreed that no one could understand what it was.

On the floor of Congress in Washington, speakers talked at length about the fact that "only twelve men in the world today may understand what the Einstein theory is all about."

Albert claimed that the basic principles involved could be understood by any earnest, conscientious second-year physics student. He encouraged the young men who studied with him, and even others who were not in his classes, to come to him for explanation of his theory, or any other problem they might be having difficulty with in the field of mathematics or physics, for that matter.

"If you have a problem, come to me with it," he said over and over again. "You will never disturb me, since I can interrupt my own work at any moment."

It didn't take long for the word to get around the Princeton campus. Old Albert meant what he said! He was never too busy to help a fellow with his homework even if the guy wasn't even in his class. More than that, the little woolly-haired scientist with the flapping tan cardigan sweater or the buttoned-up leather windbreaker—depending on the season of the year—would never be too busy to listen to problems that had nothing whatever to do with math or physics, but were concerned with how to get home for the weekend without any money for train fare or how to get a date in Philadelphia. The undergrads at Princeton bet each other that the Professor would undertake anything. But too many students lost their bets, and after a while no one would bet against Albert Einstein.

During these early years at Princeton, Albert seemed to be driven by two great forces. He wanted to have as many people as possible understand his theory of relativity and he wanted to discourage everyone from thinking about the smashing of the atom and the release of vast forces which seemed to be beyond control.

"The world isn't ready for it yet," he used to say every time some advanced student or inventor approached him with the idea that he should do more research and experimentation on nuclear fission. "There's plenty of time for that," he'd say and change the subject.

Quite the opposite was his attitude about relativity which, in a way, was directly responsible for the whole idea that there was energy in matter waiting to be released. No one had to ask twice for an explanation of the theory of relativity. His many explanations varied with the audience he was addressing. If he were talking to a group of science students he might explain in technical terms the fact that everything in the universe—every planet, the sun, the moon, earth—was constantly in motion and that therefore the position of each planet was changed from moment to moment in relation to the others, and that hence one could obtain a relative finding of their positions but not a definite fixed point on the map at which any one planet could always be found.

Or he might draw a diagram on the blackboard explaining that it represented an airplane in flight.

"Imagine that where the bomb bay is usally placed, we have inserted a hundred-foot piece of transparent pipe extending downward from the floor of the plane.

"Now suppose there is a man seated at the opening of this pipe in the plane. He takes a black marble and drops it into the pipe. He peers down the pipe and watches the marble fall through. To this man it seems that the marble falls straight down in an absolutely perpendicular course, confined as it is by the circular walls of the pipe. Plain, so far?"

Everyone in the class nods. It is certainly understandable up to this point.

"Actually," the Professor continues with a slight smile, "any observer on the ground would call the man in the plane a liar.

"The plane is moving from your right to your left, so that to the ground observer it seems as if the marble falls in a slanting trajectory. Which observer sees the truth? The answer, of course, is both!"

Sometimes, when he was addressing a group of college freshmen who had no real hope of ever understanding the Einstein theory of relativity, and frankly didn't allow it to bother them too much, Albert would resort to a quick joke to catch their interest.

"When you are sitting with a pretty girl on your lap an hour seems like a minute. But if you put your finger on a hot stove a minute seems like an hour. That is relativity."

But best of all, Albert Einstein loved to discuss his theory with those who were not scientists or even would-be scientists but were just nice, everyday people. He enjoyed helping friends and visitors understand the relationship of his mathematical theory to everyday living, and in order to do so he would often tell in his own words a story by the famous French author Anatole France.

He told them the story of the good man who went everywhere in search of the Truth. Nothing would satisfy him but the final, the Absolute Truth about everything: life, death, good, evil —everything. Finally an angel took pity on this man who in all his searching had never felt certain that what he saw and what he read was really true. The angel took this man to a secret chamber far below the surface of the earth, and there he showed him a strange contraption.

It was huge, a tremendous wheel, bigger than any wheel the man had ever seen before. Between the spokes of the wheel, and clinging to them with both hands, stood men and women of every race and every color that the man had ever heard of. As he and his guiding angel approached the wheel, all these people—every last one of them—began shouting and crying aloud in his own language. Of course, the man couldn't understand all of them, but those whose languages he could understand were all saying, "I, and I alone, speak the truth! My neighbor here is lying. *I* speak the truth."

The man turned in great uncertainty to the angel.

"But if one of them is speaking the truth, all the rest must be wrong!" he exclaimed. "How can that be? And if it be so, then which one is speaking the truth?"

The angel smiled.

"None of them speaks the Truth," the angel announced.

The man was really frightened now.

"You mean," he asked, his voice trembling, "that there is no Truth?"

"Who knows?" the angel answered. "If one has faith—listen!"

With that he caught the rim of the great wheel in both his hands and gave it a whirl with all his strength. It began to turn, slowly at first, then faster and faster. And as it moved, from the mouth of every man and woman clutching the spokes came the cry of "I speak the truth. My neighbor lies. Don't listen to him. *I* speak the truth."

Then, as the wheel turned faster and faster the man noticed that all the faces between the spokes seemed to blend into one great blur in which no one face was distinguishable and the noise grew louder and louder and the word "Truth" seemed clearer and suddenly a white light seemed to come from all the faces as they flashed past and it filled the room and the sound that came from the wheel was the sound of Truth.

The man turned to the angel and cried out in gratitude.

"Oh, thank you! Thank you for letting me see and hear. There is a Truth! I know it now! There is an Absolute Truth."

"If you believe there is, there is," the angel answered smiling.

"But isn't that the Truth?" the man cried out, for he was frightened again. "It has the ring of Truth."

"It may well be," the angel answered. "At least it is the closest to it we have been allowed to come so far."

That was one of Albert Einstein's favorite ways of explaining his theory of relativity as it pertained to philosophy and the world of ideas.

"The only way anyone can approach the truth is if everyone seeks it, and if everyone cries out when he thinks he has found it. Then each time the wheel is turned we will get a little closer to the truth—if there is such a thing."

Dr. Einstein had not been at Princeton very long before he realized that he had abandoned another idea that he had been loyal to for a very long time.

His friend Friedrich Adler, whom he had saved from the firing squad, had spent the whole period between World War I and World War II in prison. He was released only to be sent to a concentration camp as a Jew. This example of German injustice and persecution caused Albert to abandon all thought of non-resistance and pacifism.

"Since the arrival of the fascist danger, I do not believe in passive pacifism for the present. As long as fascism rules in Europe, there will be no peace."

He had every reason to believe that at that time fascism was very far from being defeated in Europe. It was a threat, a growing menace to his race and to every idea of relative philosophy to which he had devoted most of his life.

In Berlin, at the Kaiser Wilhelm Institute, there were several of his former students and colleagues who had been working for years on the development of energy from matter. They had discovered that the mineral known as uranium was most likely to produce such energy.

Two former students in particular were far ahead of the field in their experiments. They were Otto Hahn and Lise Meitner. Dr. Einstein had always regarded Miss Meitner as even a greater physicist than Madame Curie. Hahn and Lise Meitner were the first to discover that the uranium atom can be broken down or "smashed," thus releasing energy. It was Miss Meitner alone who discovered that a set of chain reactions could be set up—a series of explosions as each unit of energy was released, with each explosion many times bigger than the one before it.

Through loyal friends, Lise Meitner learned that Hitler's Gestapo was on the point of seizing her, and sending her to one of the many horrible concentration camps. Ironically, they ignored the fact that she was a great scientist on the very verge of discovering a great new force, a force that might have won the war for Germany. They didn't know of her experiments and research. They only knew that she was Jewish.

Hahn and other friends and co-workers managed to smuggle Lise Meitner out of Germany with all her notes and notebooks, but very little in the way of clothes or money. Once safely in Denmark, the courageous woman scientist sought out Dr. Niels Bohr, director of the Copenhagen Institute of Theoretical Physics.

Dr. Bohr became intensely excited by Lise Meitner's notes. With Dr. Rutherford in England he had studied the atom and Dr. Einstein's formula, $E=mc^2$, as applied to it. He knew that Enrico Fermi, an Italian refugee who had fled to America, had followed up some of

Lise Meitner's experiments on chain reactions. Soon Bohr smuggled Lise Meitner's notes across the ocean to Fermi.

Lise Meitner's findings indicated that as much energy could be released by a pound of uranium as by the burning of many thousands of tons of coal.

Scientists had become convinced that it would be possible to produce uranium bombs with millions of times the destructive power of previously known explosives.

Fermi was working at Columbia University with a physicist named Szilard, a Hungarian Jewish refugee from the University of Berlin. They realized that atomic bombs could be made, but they knew it would take months to set up the necessary laboratories, and possibly longer to train the necessary scientists and workers. They hesitated to put the matter before the Army or State Department. The whole idea of the atom bomb was so vast that they thought the project might be disregarded. They were afraid that they would be considered only as a couple of crackpot professors.

The President of the United States himself seemed to be the only answer. Franklin Delano Roosevelt had shown time and again that he had a great deal of respect for college professors. Szilard and Fermi decided to ask Dr. Einstein to either write or see the President. They realized the need for secrecy and instead of writing directly to Einstein, they wrote to Eugene Wigner, a Czech physicist who was also on the faculty at Princeton. On an August morning in 1939 they boarded a train headed for Princeton, and an interview with the discoverer of the formula which had led to the eventual production, someday, of an atom bomb.

Hours later they sat in the charming garden in back of Albert Einstein's home and told him about Lise Meitner and about her work in splitting the atom.

"So you can see," Fermi concluded, "that it's necessary for us to get in touch with President Roosevelt. Will you write to him or seek an interview?"

Albert Einstein hesitated. He looked out over his pleasant garden, and allowed his thoughts to wander while the two impatient young physicists watched him anxiously. He was not looking at the garden. He was thinking of his school days and of what he and his family had suffered under German militarism. He saw himself and Friedrich Adler as young men discussing with deadly earnestness the great need for pacifism. Then he recalled the night in the Patent Office in Berne when his formula, $E=mc^2$, had suddenly emerged from the many figure-covered sheets of paper on the desk before him. At that moment—and many times since, but especially when Lise Meitner became his student—he had realized, perhaps subconsciously, that someday he would have to decide whether he wanted to assume responsibility for the creation of the most terrible weapon of destruction ever conceived.

Fermi's Italian temperament could stand the strain no longer. He leaned forward in the wicker garden chair so that it creaked and squeaked complainingly.

"Will you write the President?" he asked.

"Would it do any good?" the Professor asked simply. "We have never met. He doesn't know me."

They smiled in relief.

"Everyone, including the President, knows and admires you."

But still Albert Einstein hesitated. He had come, he knew, to the real crossroads of his life. He had tried to avoid this decision, but he had failed. Now he asked one more question that he thought might help him to decide.

"What became of Otto Hahn?" he asked.

The two young men were taken by surprise. "Why—why—"

"Is he still at the Kaiser Wilhelm Institute?"

"As far as we know, he—"

"Working with our Lise, he may have found out everything. Have there been any large shipments of uranium to Germany recently?"

"Yes, we were going to tell you. There—"

Professor Einstein pushed himself up from the wide wicker chair. There was weariness in his manner but no more hesitation.

"I will write the letter," he said, and started off in the direction of his study.

August 2nd, 1939

F. D. Roosevelt,
President of the United States,
White House
Washington, D.C.

Sir:

Some recent work by E. Fermi and L. Szilard, which has been communicated to me in manuscript, leads me to expect that the element uranium may be turned into a new and important source of energy in the immediate future. Certain aspects of the situation which has arisen seem to call for watchfulness and, if necessary, quick action on the part of the Administration. I believe therefore that it is my duty to bring to your attention the following facts and recommendations:

In the course of the last four months it has been made probable through the work of Joliot in France as well as Fermi and Szilard in America—that it may become possible to set up a nuclear chain reaction in a large mass of uranium, by which vast amounts of power and large quantities of new radium-like elements would be generated. Now it appears almost certain that this could be achieved in the immediate future.

This new phenomenon would also lead to the construction of bombs, and it is conceivable—though much less certain—that extremely powerful bombs of a new type may thus be constructed. A single bomb of this type, carried by boat and exploded in a port, might very well destroy the whole port together with some of the surrounding territory. However, such bombs might very well prove to be too heavy for transportation by air.

. . . .

I understand that Germany has actually stopped the sale of uranium from the Czechoslovakian mines which she has taken over. That she should have taken such early action might be understood on the ground that the son of the German Under-Secretary of State, von Weizsäcker, is attached to the Kaiser-Wilhelm-Institute in Berlin where some of the American work on uranium is now being repeated.

Yours very truly,
/s ALBERT EINSTEIN
/t (Albert Einstein)

Chapter 11

ATOMS TO DESTROY

ALTHOUGH President Roosevelt's response was immediate, and leading physicists were summoned at once, the Manhattan Project, as it came to be known, did not succeed in the manufacture of a single bomb until more than five years later.

On July 16, 1945, the first test of the bomb took place in a remote section of the Alamogordo Reservation in New Mexico. The bomb was to be dropped from a steel tower. Around it, the area had been cleared for many miles. The first observation post was erected six miles from the explosion site.

Ten miles away, the scientists waited. Those who headed the Manhattan Project were there, and a small group of scientists including Einstein, Fermi and Szilard had been invited. There was tremendous tension as the countdown began: "Minus 20 minutes . . . minus 10 minutes . . . minus 5 minutes . . ." At minus 45 seconds, the robot mechanism took control.

Those last few seconds must have seemed like hours . . . "three . . . two . . . one . . . zero!"

The bomb struck.

A flash, much brighter than brightest daylight, lit up the whole area. The mountain range three miles away was brought into clear focus. There was a deafening, sustained roar, and a tremendous pressure wave swept outward in a great circle, knocking over two men who had stepped outside the bunker. Then, with incredibly lazy slowness, a multicolored surging cloud billowed from the ground like a huge animal awakening and stretching after a winter's hibernation. The cloud continued to rise and spread as it mounted higher and higher toward the sky. Gradually, as it reached its peak, the colors faded to a dull and deadly gray, and the stratospheric winds began to disperse the boiling mass.

"How soon will it be safe to drive over there?" someone asked.

"Not for at least twenty-four hours," one of the scientists said. "We've no way of telling how long the area will remain infected—perhaps permanently. But we should be able to get a look through our glasses in about twenty minutes."

As they waited, the black mist seemed to lift as if they were being offered a private viewing of a new site or the unveiling of a new monument.

There was literally total destruction. Not a

tree, not a house, not a hill, was left where it had been. There was just a vast crater and mile after mile of black rubble. The group on the platform remained frozen for a moment in awe-struck silence.

It was Dr. Einstein who spoke first.

"Our generation," he said, "has brought into the world the most revolutionary force since prehistoric man's discovery of fire."

Horror held all the scientists. It was one thing to have figured on paper the tremendous force of nuclear explosion and the destruction it would cause, but the actual sight of such complete devastation over so large an area gave Fermi and Szilard the feeling that they had opened a Pandora's box and released furies which would prove uncontrollable.

"Should this awful weapon ever be used against an enemy nation?" Fermi asked, seeing in his mind's eye the wiping out of the lovely buildings, the fountains, the seven hills themselves of his native city, Rome.

Albert Einstein smiled gently. "It does not have to be used," he said. The Army officials, the President and his aides turned to stare at him in surprise.

"Why did we spend all those millions of dollars of the taxpayers' money, if we're not going to use it?" someone asked.

"President Roosevelt was of the opinion that it would never be needed if its destructive power were what we prophesied for it."

"He believed that?"

"Not only did he believe it, but before enlisting my help he promised me that it would not be used unless everything else failed."

"Just what did he mean by everything else? The loss of more American lives? The loss of more planes and ships?"

"No," Albert Einstein replied quietly, "he said that if the weapon were truly terrifying, then a demonstration in some wasteland, like Siberia or the Aleutian Islands, would serve as well as actual killing. It was on those conditions that we have helped."

One of the Army Chiefs of Staff raised startled eyebrows. "All the time we are notifying the enemy of the demonstration, all the time we are arranging the details of it and awaiting word if they'll attend, all those weeks, American boys will be losing their lives. Wouldn't it actually save more human life to drop the bomb without warning on some desolate unimportant little island like Hiroshima, for instance?"

Einstein's cheeks flushed angrily. "Who are you to say that the people on Hiroshima are more or less important than any other people?" he asked.

"They are Japanese and they are enemies," the officer answered. "Isn't that enough?"

"Is it enough for their families?"

"There will be none left to mourn."

Einstein shook his head in anger. He felt as if he had been betrayed. It was as if, in his lifelong feud against militarist thinking, he had lost. The Army had at last beaten him.

When the A-bomb dropped on Hiroshima and three weeks later on Nagasaki on August 6, 1945, they resulted in the end of World War II. Dr. Einstein found himself hailed as the great hero of the war. He became, unwillingly, the man of the hour. In vain were his protests.

"My part in it was quite indirect," he told reporters. "I did not, in fact, foresee that atomic energy would be released in my time. I believed only that release was theoretically possible. It became practical through the accidental discovery of chain reactions, and this was not something I could have predicted."

"Dr. Einstein," one of his interviewers asked him. "Just who *did* discover the chain reactions you speak of? You said the discovery was accidental?"

Albert Einstein smiled and looked out over the lovely garden in which his wife had always spent so much time. She had died in 1938, and he missed her with a never-ending loneliness. Yet he was glad now that she had not lived to see the world become a monstrous thing with the peoples of earth ready to destroy each other for greed and power as if they had not just survived one horrible holocaust.

"It was discovered by one Otto Hahn at the Kaiser Wilhelm Institute in Berlin. He, however, completely misinterpreted what he had discovered. Had he not made this mistake the Nazis would have had the atom bomb."

"Whew!" one of the reporters whistled. "That was close. What happened?"

"It is a lovely ironic story and I shall always enjoy telling it," the great scientist said, smiling. "Hahn was working with one of my former pupils, Lise Meitner. She realized the meaning of what Hahn had discovered. For some reason she did not tell him. He was a German, an Aryan, but they were both scientists and the world of science knows no racial or national boundaries. She would have told him, except that friends rushed in to tell her that at that very moment the Gestapo was at her apartment waiting to arrest her when she returned. She was being hunted down because she was a Jewess. This was the only reason. Neither Hitler nor his Gestapo knew anything of the value of the experiments being conducted by Fräulein Meitner. Her friends helped her gather up her notes and findings as well as her interpretation of Hahn's findings, and rushed her out of Berlin. She took only her notes and the clothes she was wearing. She could not go to her apartment to get money or clothes she had there because the Gestapo was waiting there. As you know, it was while she was in Sweden that she worked out the remaining details."

"That's quite a spy story," exclaimed one of the reporters. "Do you know what happened to Hahn?"

"Yes, I know—now," Dr. Einstein said, leaning forward, still smiling. "What he had discovered seemed to dawn on him some time after Lise had escaped. I have this only on the guesses of several other colleagues of mine whom I have been able to contact since the war ended."

"He did find out, eventually, then?"

"Yes. That was when the large shipments of uranium were requested by Germany. That was what led us to believe the Nazis, too, had the needed information. But they didn't. It seems that Hitler and his officers decided that every cent of government money was needed for ground armies—long-range guns, antiaircraft and small cannon—so all that had been promised the scientists was withheld. Experiments were discontinued. The Allies got the atom bomb only by an accident—the accident that he persecuted all Jews. If he hadn't, in another day the secret would have been in German hands, and what the Nazis would have done with it is unthinkable."

There was a long silence as the interviewers sat, watching their host and each thinking his own thoughts.

"It is a great story," one of them said at last.

Another reporter, who was Jewish, spoke with deep feeling. "It is almost as if all those poor beings who perished in the gas chambers of Hitler's concentration camps have been avenged by one small Jewish girl and her professor—"

"Don't say avenged," Dr. Einstein said sharply. "There was nothing of vengeance in Lise's thoughts or in mine. Not at any time!"

The reporter apologized, and Albert Einstein leaned back in his chair.

"There was no vengeance, but there is now the feeling that the spirits of those poor degraded dead people have been appeased and that they may at last rest in peace."

"I gather," another reporter said quickly, "that you'd not have written to President Roosevelt at all, if you hadn't believed that Hitler was about to begin making the A-bomb?"

"Had I known that they wouldn't succeed in developing it, I would have done nothing–absolutely nothing. And believe me, gentlemen, there are many times that I wonder whether what I did was right. Do you realize that in another war, the use of the atomic bombs might wipe out two-thirds of all the people on this earth?"

Chapter 12

ATOMS TO HEAL

HE WAS seventy when he retired from the Institute for Advanced Study at Princeton. But as he had spent so many happy years there and the house with the big garden held so many memories for him, he decided to stay on and continue his work on his "field theory" of space from this lovely spot.

His sister, Maja, not too well now, loved being with him and enjoyed having him read aloud to her, much as their father had read aloud to them both at home in Munich. His loyal and loving friend and secretary, Helen Dukas, who had been with him for so many years, continued to take dictation, separate his notes into classifications and file them under the proper subject.

To those closest to him it seemed that for some time after his retirement he was depressed by the sense of responsibility he felt for the use of the atom bomb at Hiroshima and for the further and even more dreadful use in other wars. Then one day, suddenly and without any indication that it was coming, a change became noticeable in him. There was a greater spring to his step. He resumed his habit of taking the dog Chico for long walks. The undergraduates of Princeton were delighted to behold the once familiar figure crossing the campus again as gaily as ever. A group of boys, seeing him coming toward them, began singing a song that had been written years before when he first came to Princeton:

"Oh, the bright boys they all study math—
studee math—
And Albie Einstein points the path—
points the path—
Although he seldom takes the air—
We wish to God he'd cut his hair."

The very dignified Herr Doktor Albert Einstein, who could have paraded an astonishing number of letters after his name to indicate even a partial list of his honorary degrees, Nobel Prize winner, scientist extraordinary, grinned like a freshman, and in passing, made a very undignified gesture which brought a howl of delight from the undergraduates.

Still smiling, he rounded the campus on his way home. He realized he felt at least ten years younger. He had decided that his usefulness to the world was not a thing of the past. There was much he could still do . . . much he could still do. But—first of all—he knew he must stop thinking of himself as an old man. He must stop living in the past, weighed down by a sense of responsibility for the devastation his formula had caused. He knew now that he must think only of the future. There was so much to be done. He regretted the time he had wasted in sorrow and self-criticism. From now on, every minute must be put to constructive use. Quickly he formulated a two-point program.

First, he must lead the way in showing his fellow scientists some of the innumerable peacetime uses of atomic power. Second, he must help to evolve a plan to control its destructive potential.

He began writing articles for popular as well as scientific magazines. He visited physicists and physicians and invited many to visit him at Princeton. And soon announcements began appearing in the newspapers—at first in small articles buried in the back pages, but eventually proclaimed proudly in blazing headlines:

RADIOACTIVE IODINE MAY PROVE EFFECTIVE IN TREATMENT OF GOITER

NEUTRON BEAM USED AS CANCER CURE

ATOM RESPONSIBLE FOR CURE OF BONE DECAY

In response to Albert Einstein's provocative articles, the medical profession gladly answered the challenge to develop therapeutic uses for radiation and isotopes. Scientists, too, rose to the occasion. As a result, new, better, and less expensive methods of heating and lighting were soon discovered. Nutrition complements and better food values were developed. The cost of transportation was reduced because of scientific experiments with new fuels. There was every indication that the world would one day be a better, happier place because of the harnessing of the atom.

But this was not enough for Albert Einstein. There was the second—and, to him, equally important part of his program. This was to show the civilized world the complete horror of atomic or nuclear warfare and so discourage its use. To implement this plan, Albert hoped to interest men of good-will everywhere to serve on a Commission to plan the control of atomic weapons by a world-wide organization, enforcing its decision by a world police force.

"The very menace of nuclear warfare may—and must be made to—intimidate the human race into bringing order into its international affairs, which, without the pressure of fear, it would not do," he wrote. He put aside his inherent shyness and forced himself to meet the men in high places who could help. He spoke at banquets, at dinners, at meetings. Believing that most important of all was the teaching of these ideas to young people who would grow up in the "atomic age," he even became a member of the faculty of Brandeis College so as to have the authority of a teacher to add to his status as a scientist. Truman, Baruch, Eisenhower, Churchill, Adenauer, among other prominent figures in the world of politics and ideas, fell under his spell. He was particularly drawn to President Eisenhower who, he felt, was like himself. Eisenhower, coming from a family of Quakers who hated war, loathing it himself, had nevertheless been forced by ironic circumstances to become one of the world's best-known soldiers.

The years that followed saw the growth and development of the United Nations with the sort of international atomic control that Albert had envisioned. They saw, too, thousands of boys and girls in every part of the world turning to the study of the peace-time uses of nuclear physics. During those years, Albert Einstein himself seemed to have become a space-man. He was everywhere. Addressing a university in Oregon one day, and a meeting of a Rotary Club in Worcester the next. His activities seemed to increase with each passing day. In his lifetime he had become a legend. No one thought of him as being mortal.

On April 18, 1955, the whole world gasped at the news that screamed from headlines and was heard on radio and TV wherever there were newspapers or antennae. Albert Einstein was dead at seventy-six.

President Dwight D. Eisenhower said: "No other man contributed so much to the vast expansion of twentieth-century knowledge. Yet no other man was more modest in the possession of the power that is knowledge, more sure that power without wisdom is deadly. To all who live in the nuclear age, Albert Einstein exemplified the mighty creative ability of the individual in a free society."

Einstein had been quite wrong about one thing. It was something he had said half-jokingly when he was a young man. As it turned out, the Swiss claimed him as a Swiss, the Germans claimed him as a German, the Jews claimed him as a Jew. Moreover, the Riverside Church in New York, by placing his statue in its hall of fame, claimed him as a great scientist and humanitarian, but more important to him would have been the knowledge that everyday people —barbers and workmen and farmers and bankers and children—these mourned his passing as a friend and as a great man.